McGowan's Pass

Also by Rob Smith:

Novels:
Children of Light
McGowan's Call
McGowan's Retreat
McGowan's Return
Shrader Marks: Keelhouse

Criticism:
Hogwarts, Narnia, and Middle Earth

Poetry:
256 Zones of Gray
Mzungu, Hello
The Immigrant's House

McGowan's Pass

Rob Smith

Drinian Press/
Huron, Ohio

This book is a work of fiction. As such, names, characters, incidents, and places (real or imagined) are used fictitiously and are products of the author's imagination. Any resemblance to persons or actual events is coincidental.

Copyright © 2012 by Robert Bruce Smith
All rights reserved. No part of this book may be scanned, reproduced, or distributed in printed or electronic form without permission.

Cover photo: Washburn Ditch south of Cleveland Road

Drinian Press, LLC
P.O. Box 63
Huron, Ohio 44839
Visit our Web site at: www.DrinianPress.com

Library of Congress Control Number: 2012954224

Smith, Rob- 1947

ISBN-10: 0983306958
ISBN-13: 978-0-9833069-5-5

Printed in the United States of America

McGowan's Pass

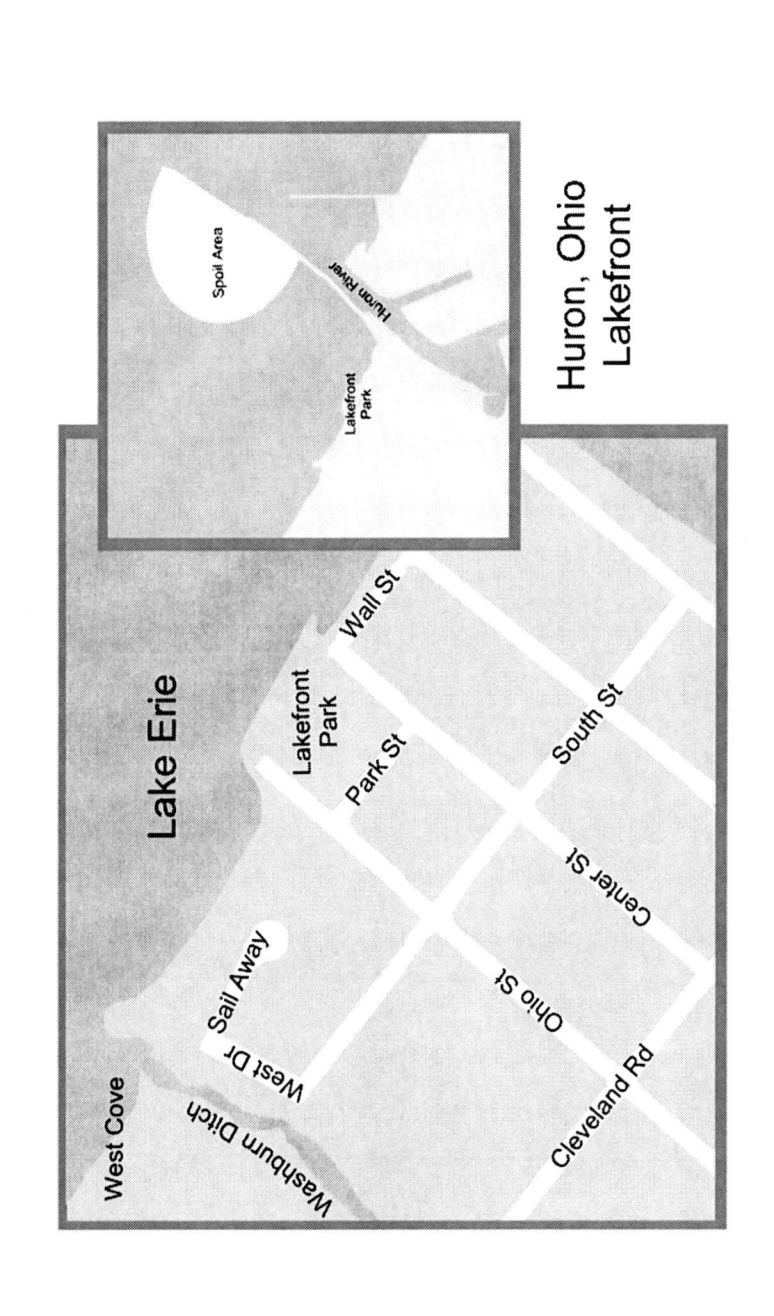

Huron, Ohio Lakefront

Chapter 1

The Quarterback and the Geek

The waters of the small bay were calm, and it was an easy paddle out to the tip of the peninsula where he had left his partner minding the gear. As he approached the broken slabs of concrete that lined the shore, a powerboat anxious to make harbor, threw up a wake that caused the light boat to roll violently toward the rocky sill.

"Hey, Airhead, this isn't the best place to try and land a canoe."

"What are you doing here? And the name is Aaron."

"Oh, it's just a friendly nickname! I was fishing near the point, and saw you hit by that prop wash. I'm just offering to lend a hand to a classmate, anything wrong with that? Hey, if you don't need any help, well, it's up to you, but you'll rip the bottom of that thing if you try to pull it over the rocks. Do you have a rope you can throw me?"

Aaron looked warily at the teen who was offering to help him ashore. "I don't really want to pull it ashore; I was just going to grab the gear that I have there. Been fishing from the rocks and thought it'd be better on the water. No waves tonight, I thought the canoe would be safe enough."

"Good thinking. If you load everything in it, you can beach it over at West Cove later. That way, when you're done you won't have to carry all the stuff back over the breakwall to your car."

Aaron looked back across the shallow bay. He had carried the canoe down to the beach at Lakefront Park; or rather he had rolled it on the dolly that was the out-of-water storage platform for the light boat. He had borrowed the canoe from his grandfather who lived just two blocks from the public beach. The shore off West Drive was a more private beach, and the known party-place among high schoolers. As he looked over his shoulder, he could see that it was glowing with the light of one campfire and was already populated by a few shapes of people his own age getting into a party mood. They were the in-crowd, and probably not receptive to let in a geek with hands that smelled freshly of fish.

"Didn't drive," said Aaron, who was somewhat wary of the sudden interest being shown to him by the suspiciously helpful quarterback of the football team. Still, this was not the place to try to hold off a rocking aluminum canoe against the riprap of limestone boulders.

"Come on, just give me a line," came a more insistent request. "At least I can get you alongside and fend you off until you get loaded."

Aaron looked around the tiny boat. The only ropes he had were a short painter tied off on the bow and a twenty-five foot coil with one end tied to the thwart just in front of him and half of a cement block on the other. It was an unorthodox anchor, but one that had always served him well in the shallows off the southwest end of the spoil area.

He went to work on the knot that held the lighter end. It was a proper bowline, the "King of Knots" as his grandfather often said—"always hold tight when you need 'em, and untie easily when you don't." Aaron's fingers made quick work of the release.

"Here," he said tossing the coil to his newly found partner. He was confident that the weighted end would stay firmly grounded near his feet. It did, at least initially. What he had not anticipated was the vigorous tug that pulled him hard against the rocks and tumbled him into the water.

Though the water was only a few feet deep, he resurfaced with a sputter and a gasp. Even through his water bleary eyes, he could see that the canoe had been pulled up out of the water. What he also saw was the athletic rotation of a piece of concrete on the end of a rope. It swung around like a hammer thrown at a track and field event, but it was pivoting toward his skull.

"Sorry, Airhead, but I need to borrow your boat."

Chapter 2

Paris en Novembre

Beth had finally shutdown her e-reader and was sleeping quietly in the seat next to Davis. They were nearing the end of a long holiday, and the whole thing was not fully in perspective. Probably wouldn't be for a long time. On the other hand, two nights in Paris had proved a wise precaution against a full seventeen hours in the air that would have been the more direct flight home from Nairobi.

There was a huge contrast between two cities, Paris and Eldoret in western Kenya. Nairobi would have made a closer comparison to the French capitol, but life in the more rural regions of the country provided only differences. It was not a place frequented by foreign travelers, *mzungu* in the Kiswahili language, but the McGowans' itinerary was preconditioned by an anthropologist daughter and her family living *in situ* for the year. As it turned out, the three November weeks they spent visiting grandchildren also introduced them to two Africas, the one of the tourists and the one of the people.

He knew the visit to the tribal regions would have deep-seated appeal to his friends from the College Hill Church in Dayton. There, people longed to know their African connections. In Kenya, he had discovered hospitality in the homes of the Luo, Kikuyu, Maasai, Kalenjin, and clans such as the Nandi. These were the friends and co-workers of his daughter and colleagues in the effort to stop AIDS from decimating traditional families. The intelligence and energy of these people brought hope, but it was an optimism tempered by a visit to Neema House, a residential school filled with children orphaned by the disease, many, who bore the virus as their birthright.

Africa is a hard place, he thought. *I don't know many Americans who could cut it.* That was the conclusion that he arrived at by day two. Every man he met described himself as a mechanic, and he soon realized why when he saw two men replacing the rear end of a Toyota pickup on the side of a dirt road. At home, there'd be a call to a garage and they'd sent out a tow. In Africa, if you can't fix it yourself, you don't have it anymore.

The roads were another thing. Many might have been simply rutted paths aspiring to be roads, but the drivers drove them by straddling eroded crevasses with an eye to match a narrow wheelbase to the edges of a canyon deep enough to swallow the car. Africa was not a place for the fainthearted.

Davis feared, however, that the survival skills of the locals were not so easily transferable to the western world of insatiable consumers. The American way was to complain and throw cash. The Kenyan way was to find a way with no cash to throw.

Some words continued to haunt McGowan. They were not, however, the words of important conversations. They were the throwaway sidebars of casual interactions. He remembered talking to a young guard at the gate of the compound. He spoke perfect English, and Davis also knew he'd have at least two other languages,

Kiswahili and his tribal language, on some hypothetical *vitae*.

McGowan had been walking with his grandchildren within the gated community that sheltered western visitors and NGO workers. They had insisted that Ima come along. She was their favorite tutor who was, herself, studying for university entrance exams. I introduced them all to the guard, a man, perhaps in his late twenties.

"Ima is hoping to go to university next semester," Davis bragged. The young woman smiled proudly.

"So you still have dreams?" said the guard.

Dreams, thought McGowan, who could not imagine living without them. Dreams were more at home in the tourist's Africa. He and Beth had walked among the zebras and wildebeests on Crescent Island where *Out of Africa* was filmed. They had motored across Lake Naivasha to get there, seeing hippos in route and stopping to see a local showing off a gigantic carp that he hoped to sell in the market. All that belonged to beautiful, wild Africa that showed up in *National Geographic*, but was largely unseen by rural natives who carried six-foot stacks of cordwood on bicycles or walked with large sacks of maize balanced on heads.

Infrastructure is sketchy in Kenya, politicians often corrupt, and the people pay for both. Davis had intended to keep a journal during the trip, but the narrative was too emotional for anything except poetry. He opened his notes and read an entry:

Eldoret

At night they close the
black grillwork over the
front door. It clangs shut

ending with a solemn
click.
Only the first night alarming, soon
becoming the ritual sound of darkness
signaling sleep soon to come
to a house
gated in a cluster of gated houses
sealed round by cinderblock walls
topped with electrified barbed wire,
surrounded again with
another gated perimeter–
and making my bed the inner doll
of a *Matryoshka,*
where I sleep
free in Africa
with three iron gates
and three block walls
between me and the street
where tomorrow bundles
of old clothes and shoes
will be spilled out
on the dirt pathway for sale,
and I will walk past without need,
trying not to see,
never tempted to buy.

But tonight, the dogs
inside the compound walls
bark me awake.
Are they just talking to the guards,
practicing,
or do they see desperate
shadows on the wall?
I wonder as I sleep
free in Africa.

Beth had liked Paris, but to Davis, the frantic consumerism seemed to only highlight the humanity of the African experience. The bed in the hotel provided recovery, however, and facing the second leg of the flight home was much easier for it.

Chapter 3

McGown's Pass

The ideal itinerary has layovers that allow enough time for catching connecting flights without any extended sitting at the gate. The two-day layover in Paris meant that there was no rush to another gate, just the limo ride to the hotel which was a block from the *Arc d' Triomphe*. JFK was another issue.

When the flight had been booked, warning red text on the computer screen warned that switching gates in New York also meant switching terminals for the final leg to Cleveland. This would be in addition to passing through the customs and immigration check points. *Forty-five minutes* sounded like a sprint with suitcases.

"International flights usually arrive early" was the closest thing to an assurance that the ticket agent could give, but *usually* was no guarantee. Then she also explained that the flight they would be bumped to (along with how many other passengers?) was the last of the day. Missing that or discovering it was already at capacity meant a night in NYC. As intriguing as that might have been for some, it was a budget buster after a trip that had already burdened the McGowans' checkbook. They booked the later flight to guarantee sleeping in their own bed after nearly a month on two other continents.

The four-hour layover, however, was rescued before the ink on their e-ticket printout had long to dry. It came in the form of a telephone call from Matt Fornesby.

Matt had been a teenager at Covenant Church when McGowan served there as the pastor. That was now twenty-five years in the past. The boy was a man now, and he had followed his wife's career when she joined the medical staff at University Circle Hospitals in Cleveland. When Matt and Erin appeared in the congregation of Old First Church on Public Square, Davis and Beth thought that they had gone full-circle and the past was catching up with them. Maybe it was.

A few days after McGowan told the pair that he was headed to Africa to see his daughter, Matt called to get more specifics about the itinerary.

"I'm really not planning to stalk you, Dr. McGowan," he said over the phone. "I mentioned to my Dad that you were going and he said that's about the time he was going to be in New York City."

How likely is it that we'll run into each other? thought Davis at the time. *Twenty-some million people spread out over some seven thousand square miles and we'll be tucked in behind a security gate among people heading toward Cleveland, Ohio.*

The one thing he had not counted on was Barker Fornesby, a Chicago-based businessman with more pull than a harbor tug. He was reminded of it a few days later, when a familiar voice on the other end of the line *(are smart phones on line?)* made an offer.

"Davis? This is Barker. How are you and Beth doing these days? Matt says that you're headed to Africa."

"Yes, we are. Our little girl is studying AIDS transmission in tribal regions."

"How did they grow up on us so fast?" said Fornesby.

"They just do, don't they? Matt and Erin are a great couple, by the way."

"None of the baby books ever pointed out that the best part of parenting comes when your children grow up and become your peers," observed Barker. "They cover toilet training, adolescence, and emptying the nest, but not liking the adults they become."

"I suppose it's only if you manage to do it right," agreed McGowan.

"Or you're very lucky! Speaking of luck, I hear you have a long layover at Kennedy."

"But isn't that *bad* luck?" bantered Davis to his old friend.

"Who are you? The McGowan I used to know was an optimist. Whatever happened to the lemons and lemonade sermon?"

"That line was born a cliché. I don't think I *ever* preached that one!"

"Probably not, but how 'bout if I make it a Long Island ice tea? Molly and I are flying back from JFK to Chicago that night. I'd like for you to meet her. Let me take you to dinner on the concourse between flights."

"Highly priced fast airport food doesn't sound like your usual fare, Barker."

"We might be able to do better," said Fornesby, "if not, I'm willing to slum it. You'll be arriving at Terminal Four and switching to Eight. We'll meet you when you get off the shuttle. I assume that you haven't changed a bit, and I'll recognize you."

"Beth hasn't changed," said Davis, "but I'll wear a red carnation."

"Don't bother, then. You'll be the old man with Beth!"

The entire conversation was short and to the point. It reminded McGowan of both Fornesby's directness and why he liked this man who had a knack for getting things done. Now that he and Beth were on the way home from Paris the idea of having something to do for the four hours of gate-time seemed a nice gift as was the *interview* when they passed through customs. The agent asked about their trip and, though Davis understood that they were really being screened for security and contraband, the official managed to make it seem like a *welcome home* conversation.

"Only one percent of Americans go to Africa," he had noted. Of course, the McGowans' had additional motivations beyond the desire to see another continent. Currently, their daughter and two grandchildren were there!

"Beth!" said a voice to their right when they entered Terminal Eight. It was Barker Fornesby. "Where's Davis?" he added as a continuation of the phone banter.

"Very funny," said McGowan in answer. The two shook hands and then Fornesby stepped back beside an auburn haired woman who was standing nearby.

"This is Molly," he said. "Molly, this is Beth and Davis." The woman extended her hand to McGowan.

"I feel like I have known you for quite a while," she said, "Erin was really impressed when she and Matt had lunch with you last year."

Erin told you, not Matt, thought Davis, but he said, "She is an impressive woman. They seem like a great fit."

"They are," she agreed. Davis had never met Molly, Barker's second wife. He had, however, done the funeral for Angie, Fornesby's first wife. Her death still created tension in the family that probably had nothing to do with Molly. From his years of experience, maybe from his personal life experience, Davis had learned to recognize that death divides parents and children in different ways. A grieving spouse gets to the point where they are ready to move ahead and regain life. The children feel that they are losing the surviving parent to an intruder. Sometimes they are right, because the intruder literally wants the past buried and with it memories too precious to lose, though painful to recall.

"So how was Africa?" began Fornesby as he led the foursome away from the ramp toward a destination that McGowan could only guess. The odd thing was that they appeared to be leaving the main traffic area of the concourse where the eateries were all centered.

"I've decided that living in Africa is beyond the ability of most Americans." After making the statement, Davis was surprised by the ensuing short conversation. He assumed that Barker would do as others always had, that is, turn the discussion to the *National Geographic* wildlife version of the continent. Instead, he asked about health issues.

"I know what you mean," he began. "Did you have to worry about malaria where you were?"

"We slept under nets, but we were at altitude. The mosquitoes weren't a big problem."

"So you weren't in the basin of the Rift Valley?"

"No, we were in western Kenya, mostly centered in Eldoret. We did go to Naivasha and Nakuru on a road trip on the way back to Nairobi."

Fornesby smiled as if remembering something pleasant. "Molly and I stayed at Naberi, a little swim camp outside of Eldoret."

Now it was Davis' turn to smile. "We went there several times to swim with the grandchildren." They both had experienced the same thing and knew it. Fornesby asked the leading question.

"Did you get stares when you appeared in your bathing suits?"

McGowan turned back where Molly and Beth were engaged in their own private conversation. "Yes," he said intending to be overheard. "Everybody turned to stare, but Beth had a new bathing suit and she was hot!"

The women looked a bit confused.

"Davis has an unusual theory about why people stared at Naberi," said Barker. With this thread of an explanation the four broke out in immediate laughter. They all knew the simple truth. The local patrons were all curious about whether these *wazungu* (foreigners) were actually white *under* their clothes, too.

By the time the laughter had ended, they turned a corner and found what appeared to be an out-of-the-way elevator. They waited until the doors opened on the empty car.

"I think you'll find this a little better than the food court," offered Fornesby who slipped a plastic card with a magnetic strip into a slot just beneath the numbered pushbuttons for the first and second levels. The steel box lurched slightly as it began its ascent. When it stopped, the door in the back of the compartment slid open. To the McGowans' surprise, it emptied on a small vestibule with a podium at one end. Stationed by it was a tuxedoed *maitre d'*.

"Good evening, Mr. and Mrs. Fornesby," came the greeting, "I see that you have two guests with you. Will anyone else be joining you this evening?"

"No, William. It'll just be the four of us, thank you." He led them to a table looking out over the tarmac, and in the more distant horizon, the Atlantic.

"I think I'm a little underdressed," confessed Davis after the four had been seated.

"This is an airport," said Molly, "look around."

It was a very small dining room with only a handful of guests, some of whom nodded at the Fornesbys as they passed. The McGowans could not decide whether these were people actually acquainted with their hosts or whether they were simply familiar faces. No one nodded toward Davis or Beth, however. Molly's suggestion to *look around* also revealed that none were dressed any more formally than they. Most men wore jeans or Dockers with non-descript collared shirts. There were fewer women, and these were also dressed for comfort. The staff, on the other hand, was all formal right down to the bussers, who wore white tux shirts and black bowties.

"I don't think we're in Africa anymore, Toto," said Davis leaning toward Beth who was seated at his left.

"Are you sure?" countered Barker. "Where did you sleep at night?"

Davis then thought about the security arrangements at IU House with the gates and guards, about the need to travel only by car after dark, and the guards with AK47s who monitored the ATMs at Barclay's Bank.

"This is about safety?" he asked.

"Pretty much," said Fornesby. "Companies pay a lot of money for this façade. I see it as a reminder that when I'm leaving the country, I'm really under house arrest. Nobody wants to become a hostage, so we eat in fancy little rooms and pretend we're privileged.

"And the people that work in humanitarian programs in Africa do the same, albeit, on a less grand scale. They are not advantaged, but by comparison… well they always have money in their pockets."

The conversation flowed easily between the four. Molly and Barker had been in New York for four days to see the shows. Davis was reminded of his old friend Bryant Kirkland who had been the pastor at the Fifth Avenue Church. He had once commented that he read all the *New York Times* reviews so that he could attempt an intelligent exchange with people who could actually afford to attend the plays and concerts.

Money had its hierarchy, but Beth and Davis had laughed heartily in a two room house inhabited by an African family. Staying engaged in life was a trait that didn't parallel the commodities market. The Fornesbys had position and power and the desire to honor their humanity. They had been in the Africa that had so moved Davis.

"When did your ancestors come to North America?" asked Barker in a moment when the conversation was shifting.

"I'm second generation," said McGowan, "my grandparents immigrated here. Why?"

"No reason, except we ran into your name in Central Park. It wasn't spelled exactly the same. It was M-c-G-o-w-n, but evidently pronounced the same."

"It's a common name. Actually, it means *Smith*."

"Well, this McGown had a tavern, *The Black Horse*, in a wooded area that served as a path between a lake that's now called *Harlem Meer* and a larger marshy area."

"A tavern? Is that why you thought of me?"

Barker laughed, "You know me too well, McGowan. But it was historically important, at least the land around it was. The pass was the way up to higher ground, and Washington used it as an escape route when the British invaded Manhattan. Of course, the tavern is long gone and a convent was built on the site. That's what made me think of you!"

"Right!" said Davis.

The layover went too quickly and the Fornesbys and the McGowans took different directions to their respective gates. Davis suspected that the seating area where Barker and Molly would spend their last twenty minutes would be more posh than the long rows of back-to-back gray plastic chairs that framed their gate in Terminal Eight.

They had just claimed two side-by-side vacant seats when an announcement came over the PA. "Passenger Davis McGowan, please report to the desk at gate C32H."

He left Beth with their carry-ons as he stepped toward the man who had spoken his name over an old style wall phone near the desk.

"I'm Davis McGowan."

"Yes, Dr. McGowan. We need to make a change to your seat assignment."

He was a bit surprised that his title had been added to his name. It did not appear on his ticket. "Is something wrong?" he asked.

"No, there is no problem. It's just that we've overbooked coach and are going to have to bump you and Mrs. McGowan to first class." A new paper pass was issued and Davis went back to where Beth was waiting.

"That's never happened before," he said to his wife who was looking at him expectantly.

"What's that?" she asked.

"We've been upgraded. They said that coach was overbooked and so we've been moved to first class."

"We've been in the air a long time today," she said. "Maybe they had pity on a pair of overly-tired long-distance travelers."

"Maybe," was his noncommittal reply. His doubts were confirmed when he visited the lavatory in the economy section just after all the passengers had been boarded and the hatch was sealed. There were empty window and middle seats under the number that matched the ones on their printed itinerary.

"We need to send Barker a thank-you note," he said sliding into the roomy recliner that was his seat.

"It was a nice dinner," added Beth.

"No," he said. "We need to thank him for this first-class nap we are about to take!"

Chapter 4

Firelands College

A trip to the post office is always an adventure after a long hiatus. The McGowans found that they were claiming a huge stack of glossy catalogs pitching for holiday gifts sales. The truth was that the major part of their family celebration had already taken place in Kenya prior to Thanksgiving.

The Christmas gifts to the grandchildren were chosen on the basis of their short shelf-life rather than current market trends. In the spring when their family would finally return to the States, luggage limitations would require a choice between their daughter's research data and toys. Rather than promote confrontation, Beth and Davis brought gifts that would be used-up, broken, or left behind as gifts. Choosing presents had proved an interesting new paradigm for shopping, giving, and receiving. A dozen boxes of Kraft Macaroni and Cheese turned out to be the highlight for two children who had not found an African taste equivalent.

Most of the colorful shopping temptations from the mailbox would find their way quickly into the recycle bin in the garage. One plain 8 ½ x 11 manila envelope was far more interesting.

"Here's my contract for spring semester," said Davis as he pulled the ugly duckling from the stack of brighter plumaged cousins.

"When did it come?"

Davis looked at the postmark. "Last week," he said, "I doubt if I'll have to make an excuse for getting it in after the filing deadline." He broke the seal and saw the ten sheets of legalese that meant he would be teaching a course called *The Bible as Literature* at the Firelands College. He looked through the various forms that were highlighted and where he needed to supply information or a signature. The one that always seemed incredible was the one from Homeland Security where he had to swear that he was not a member or supporter of any terrorist organizations.

"I suppose they'd fire me for lying if my name came up on any list of subversives, but it always looks like our national security is based on the honesty of the anarchists," he said as he signed on all the dotted lines and indentured himself for a semester of eight a.m. classes on Monday, Wednesday, and Friday. Adjunct pay was pitiful for instructors and a cash-cow for the university. Students paid the same fees per credit hour, but the university paid the instructor less than half with no healthcare benefits. Davis was fortunate that he was doing this for the love of teaching and not as a means of feeding his family or trying to get a foothold in the competitive world of academia.

The money would pay for Saturday night dancing dates at Sawmill. Besides that, the teaching would keep his mind engaged, and he felt that need with winter approaching and his old duties at Old First in Cleveland now at an end.

"I'm glad you'll be teaching again," said Beth when he had sealed the return envelope.

"Want to get me out of the house?" he said back with a laugh.

"Of course! It gives me quiet mornings three days a week. What's not to love? And you'll be off raking in the dough!" They both laughed at that.

Christmas celebrations were quieter than normal with *children* scattered as far away as Montana and Africa. On the other hand, Davis had time to develop a syllabus for a campus that ran on a different academic calendar than Wright State where he had taught for years.

He found himself transitioning again, moving from the world of the parish back to the classroom. The two were so very different even though the intellectual property was the same. At Old First he was a pastor once more, involved in the life and death issues and personal crises of many people. He and Beth had survived their own crisis at that time, but, as he remembered from the past, they were on their own. Rightly or wrongly, his role was to be available to others in need, and personal issues were not allowed to distract from that function. Perhaps that is why it was such a relief to go back into the classroom. Classes were such small solar systems of narrowly focused concern. For the most part, students feared a grading system that made them comply to the absolute authority of their prof. Unlike some of his colleagues, McGowan knew it was a game. The deference shown in the classroom did not always find a home in lunchroom conversation in the Pit, as the student lounge was known.

The exceptions to the fear factor were the best part of being an educator. Watching a student transition from a grade-fearing, credit-counting individual to one awakened by the subject matter provided satisfaction that was rare in the parish.

It was an odd thing from Davis' point of view. On Sunday mornings he could preach to hundreds of people about the transforming power of faith through the movement of history and have the primary after-church conversation be whether red fruit punch should be served at coffee hour. In the classroom students listened fervently and took notes. They stayed after class with questions and were in awe of the way that learning the cultural past of the biblical era changed their opinion of the Bible. Of course, those students were generally the ones without any religious background, the ones who only knew the Bible from the stereotypical television evangelists. The religious students were a different challenge.

McGowan sometimes took the impression that the more *religious* of his students had been warned off by their local pastor to expect atheist propaganda from religious instruction at a state university. The braver ones became confused. Everything they heard from the front of the room was documented from the reference books in the library. Their instructor didn't preach. He didn't even ask them to believe. He only wanted them to understand a people in a time and a culture and how they used narrative to capture the meaning of their life experience. The irony was that he was teaching, from a neutral perspective, what his seminary professors had taught him. At the time, they were just his teachers, but over his career he saw their names on the title pages of scholarly books and in interviews in newsmagazines when a significant manuscript discovery made headlines. Metzger, Anderson, Froehlich, Migliore, and Sakenfeld were just a few who made his diploma accrue in value. What they had taught were not radical ideas of the faithless, but foundations in scholarship that made possible the old words of Davis' religious tradition: *a reasonable, religious, and holy hope.*

This had become his counter-argument with students pushing to convert him or break through with some narrower understanding of personal salvation. "Listen," he would say, "scholarship is scholarship. I am not asking you to believe anything one way or another, but I will tell you this: what I teach in this class is the product of historical, linguistic, cultural, and textual studies. This is the current state of knowledge. If you do not find a way to incorporate it into your religious understanding, you will come across as ignorant and naïve to anyone who has studied or traveled to another cultural area."

Exchange students from Africa and the Middle East seemed to have the fewest problems with his lectures. While they may not have known of the material prior to the course, they were familiar with the type of cultural setting that birthed these understandings.

Davis breathed a deep sigh.

"What was that for?" asked Beth.

"I'm looking forward to teaching, that's all."

"Getting up at six for an eight o'clock?"

"I'll grab a coffee on the way," he answered. "We can eat breakfast after class."

"You know me too well," she said.

Chapter 5

First Day of School

Firelands College is a commuter branch campus of a state university. Davis had taught several courses since his first retirement, and always found it interesting to see how the students arranged themselves on the first day. There were only twenty-two in the class, most of whom would arrive bleary-eyed and sporting a Styrofoam cup advertising the filling station nearest their home or the vending machine in the Pit.

The first to enter the room obviously had the choice of location. McGowan's theory was that they probably gravitated to the same general area in all their classes. The ones who picked the front row were often viewed as suck-ups by their peers, but Davis found that they were often the most conscientious. They wanted to see the screen and be able to ask for clarification. The back row was always a curious mix of unknowns. Some clearly wanted to be near the door, but others were *the watchers*. They wanted to see how the class would go before investing themselves in a subject that was new to them. The fact was that students were more likely to jump from the back row to the front than to settle in the middle. The late arrivers always provided comic relief as they picked their way to the most awkwardly placed empty seats.

The official catalogue number for McGowan's course was ENG324. He was teaching the Bible as literature, but had the suspicion that the *real* faculty in the English Department would approach the subject quite differently than he. They would probably use the King James text and treat the Bible as a single book. Davis' background was quite different, and he taught how time, language, and culture provide insight as to how literature shapes community. This was always a surprise to the people who assumed that American aspirations were universal traits. Here in north central Ohio there was a great deal of work to do with students who thought that a drive to Chicago was a cross-country trip and that *world travel* meant visiting a beach on the Outer Banks.

When the curtain rose on the first day of class, the first character on the stage was, as he later learned, Ashley Carpenter. From all outward appearances, she did seem a full-fledged character. She wore black. *Everything* was black from her car length pea coat and short skirt flaring out below to the high-topped combat boots on her feet. Her bare arms and legs were quite pale, and provided a complete contrast with her black lipstick and nail polish. The only variation from the theme was the silver piercings on her nose, lips, and ears. Even those seemed harmonious with the monochromatic presentation. She was a woman on a mission and took the last seat in the furthest corner of the back row.

The second arrivals were also female, and appeared to be some sort of conjoined species clad in winter-wear jackets, Bermuda shorts, and flip-flops. In spite of the fact that there was actually no snow on the ground outside, McGowan still marveled at their devotion to their fashion image. He looked out the long windows of the modern building to see the gray ominous clouds of the January sky. They took seats in the middle of the room, but not before one of the heads turned toward Ashley with a look of recognition and, what sounded like, a friendly greeting.

"Heard from your brother lately?"

The woman in black glared with practiced blankness before taking a sip of something from a lidded black ceramic mug.

From McGowan's point of view, the first day of class was always half-wasted. It required going through the syllabus and explaining aloud what was written in the packet that he had already handed to each student as they entered the room. The questions for clarification were always inane, and never as interesting as watching a round of non-Musical Chairs.

"It says that we need to write at least a three hundred word proposal for our term paper," stated one of the sisters. "Does the number of words in the title count, too?" Ashley snickered at this, but the rest of the class tuned in for an answer.

Oh, boy, thought Davis, *I'm going to have some great papers to read! At least they'll be short!* He imagined one or both of the pair trying to figure a way to expand a line of nonsense to satisfy the word count feature of their software. In his mind, he could hear an imagined dialogue: "Instead of saying that it happened a *long time ago*, you could say it was a *very* long time ago."

He didn't know if the smile that he was feeling was visible when he gave the most courteous answer he could muster. "I worry less about the actual number of words," he began, "than I do that you have a clear idea of the direction that you want to take in your research." He knew that, in their hearing, this response would be translated: *It can be less than three hundred* which would be followed by sixteen *blah-blah-blahs.*

During the succeeding days the seating arrangements shifted slightly. The front row filled, and the class, perhaps out of compassion for a disorganized few, left the seats closest to the door empty. The three initial members of the cast, in order of their appearance, remained the same, however.

As a father himself, Davis was pleased to see that flip-flops were replaced by some form of running shoe when there was actually snow on the ground, but Ashley's wardrobe seemed an inexhaustible font of darkness.

As he was packing up to leave the room, McGowan noticed that Ashley was holding back. She waited until the last of her peers cleared the space.

"Dr. McGowan," she said and Davis was pleased to learn that she actually had speech capability.

"Yes, Ashley." The woman hesitated for a moment, perhaps surprised that he knew her name.

"Dr. McGowan, I do a little writing," she began, "mostly poetry and short stories and I'm really interested in what you say about metaphor. I always thought that a metaphor was just a short figure of speech, but you are saying–at least I think you're saying–that a whole story can be a metaphor."

Davis thought about this because he didn't think that he ever quite put it that way. "I think you're on the right track," he said finally. "A narrative becomes a sort of extended metaphor. The writer's primary purpose is to point to a reality that is beyond the literal meaning of the words. As with a metaphor, if you just take the words literally, you can miss the point."

Ashley stood quietly as if rearranging ideas in her head. "Don't modern writers do the same?" she asked finally.

"Of course," said Davis. "In my opinion, the great fiction writers always do. They put a story in front of you—and it can be about anything: Orcs and hobbits and elves, for example. Take it literally, and the whole thing is silly and untrue. But there are people who read those books over and over again. Have you thought about why?"

"My parents say it's my way of escaping," she confessed, "but I think that some things are truer in fiction. I mean, there the creatures are evil or noble and you know who's who."

"Not quite like the real world, is it?" said Davis.

"Could I write my term paper on this?"

McGowan had to give this some thought, not because the topic was outrageous, but that research might prove difficult for an entry level student. "I think it could be a good paper," he said, "but, I would want to sit down with you and get very specific. If you don't have a clear focus, this could become a doctoral dissertation." He suddenly saw something that he had not expected, a smile.

"That would be so good," she said. "I'll write some ideas and show them to you. Do you think that *The Lord of the Rings* is what I should use for comparison?"

Davis felt better about giving permission. Clearly, she had recognized his reference to Tolkien. "That's one I know well," he answered, "but maybe something from C.S. Lewis or J.K. Rowling or *Hunger Games* could serve you as well."

"Thanks, Dr. McGowan," she said as she left the room less darkly than he had seen before.

Chapter 6

The Pit

Adjunct faculty at the college had no private office space where they could confer with students, so Davis arranged to meet with Ashley Carpenter in the student union, more affectionately, called *the Pit*. The appellation was due to the sunken seating area that dominated the center of a large lounge with sofas and comfortable seating. At the other end of the room was a glassed-in cafeteria with some food service, table seating, and a vending area for after hours.

Ashley, who was seated in an alcove at the far end of the room, had apparently already refilled her *noir jar* with her particular brand of flavored water, and Davis had his own Styrofoam cup from the gas station. He made his way toward where she was seated. She scanned the room nervously, but brightened when she saw his approach. *Brightened* might be an overstatement for anyone so Goth, but it was a relative description.

"Thank you for meeting with me, Dr. McGowan," she said as he pulled over another chair. She took a last furtive look over the room before turning her attention to the outline that she had prepared for her term paper.

She was a bit of a puzzle to Davis. It was not so much her actual appearance. At Wright State in Dayton he had a wide range of students that went from suits and ties to hair that mimicked parrot plumage. What was odd was her persona here in Erie County which, though a vacation Mecca in the summer, was still only a generation removed from small industries and farmland.

Ashley was well-spoken and seriously interested in learning. McGowan wondered if her wardrobe choices were more an attempt at distinction than rebellion. She understood the suggestions that he made for limiting her topic, and appreciated the fact that short papers have to be focused if they are to say anything meaningful. This was an awareness not appreciated by her classmates who saw virtue in adding generalities as a technique to expand the number of words without actually having to include content.

Her interest in her studies was Davis' motivation for getting out to the campus at eight a.m. for little pay and no long-term future. It wasn't just her. His front row crowd didn't miss a beat, and the number of students hanging around after class told him that that the subject had taken many of them by surprise. The fact was that students work from a checklist of graduation requirements. Firelands is a two-year campus, and most course offerings are designed for freshmen and sophomores. Once the basic classes were taken, students had no choice but to move over to the main campus where the cost of living and study went up. Any upper-level class offered locally would be taken, not for its interest, but as a means of meeting graduation requirements without a move or long commute. If that had been the motivation of some, many had been drawn to a world-expanding study of a different cultural way of thinking.

"What I find interesting," said Ashley, "is that I now hear things differently when I listen to the news." She took a quick glance away.

"What do you mean?" asked Davis.

"Only that all the news from the Middle East is about tribes and not just nations. I think about being an American and my loyalty is to my country. It's not that simple in the Arab world, is it?" She looked again.

"No, it isn't," agreed Davis who hardly considered himself an expert on the modern struggles. He did know, however, that the concept of nationhood was a product of the west, and ties of family and kinship were more natural in the biblical world and in the modern Arab world.

Ashley's composure posed questions for Davis. She didn't seem to have any friends on campus, but she clearly had the social graces. McGowan wondered why she continued to maintain her exile in the back row when she had far more in common with those in the front. "Why don't you change where you sit?" he asked. "The kids in the front row have a lot of little discussions before and after class. I think you'd like it." (He rued the fact that he had just used the word *kids*, but she didn't seem to take offence. Why should she? After all, he was old and even people in their thirties were starting to look younger.)

"It's easier the way it is," was all she said.

"I just thought that you'd fit in pretty well," added Davis.

"I'm not supposed to fit in… at least not around here."

The comment was filled with more hurt than bitterness, and McGowan felt she would resist any further discussion of it.

"Thank you for your help," she said and the discussion was over. Davis stood as she rose. "Could I talk with you again?" she asked, "I mean if I get stuck."

Though these last words sounded less final, it was clear that the *I-don't-feel-a-damn-thing* girl was back.

"Sure, anytime." He watched her make her way along the perimeter of the room like a dark shadow, then exit through the glass doors toward the parking lot.

Chapter 7

June Weddings

Davis reached for the phone. The caller id read *City of Lakewood*.

"Hello?"

"Dr. McGowan, this is Darnell Wilson. You may not remember me, but I was the investigator from the Lakewood PD during the Wallsoner episode."

"Of course," said Davis. "How could I forget? Is everything alright?"

"Everything is fine. I called Old First and they told me that you were no longer there. When I explained how I knew you, they gave me your home number. I hope that was okay?"

It's a breach of basic security, thought Davis. Normally Colleen would have taken Wilson's number and forwarded it to McGowan, but then, *she had met Wilson several times, the last of which was at the funeral of Bert Zacharias. At that time he was with Megan Sorento.*

"No problem," said Davis. He wanted to ask about Sorento, but thought better of risking what might have become a topic about an ex. "I hope this isn't a professional call on your part."

Darnell laughed nervously, and McGowan could envision him wearing a white dress shirt and a stylish tie. "Not professional for me," he said, "maybe for you."

"Why do I have the feeling Megan put you up to this?" He risked using her name, but if Wilson was calling to talk with a *minister* and not a person of interest, the potential subject matter was relatively limited.

"How did you know? Do you have surveillance out on me?"

"Cops and ministers," said Davis, "same line of work, aren't they?" He didn't actually believe this, but it fit the banter with a young officer that he admired for the way Darnell had conducted himself during the investigation of a serial killer in Lakewood.

"It's just that you and your wife caught us out on our first date. You told me that when I met with you at the church."

Davis did remember. "How can I help you?" he said. "You know that I owe you big time."

"You don't owe me anything," said Wilson, "but Megan and I wanted to see if you would be willing to do our wedding this June."

Davis had to pause to consider the professional ethics of the matter. "Do neither of you have a church connection, then?"

"Well, that's the problem," said Darnell. "Megan's family is Catholic and Ms. Brown belongs to the AME." (Davis didn't know who Ms. Brown was, but he knew the African Methodist Episcopal denomination.) "Anyway, we thought that we might be able to find some middle ground."

"What do your families think?"

"They're okay with it. Actually, I think Megan's folks like the idea of us being married by the water. When we heard that you actually live in Huron, well, it seemed perfect."

McGowan's mind turned on geographical references. Wilson picked up on his hesitation.

"Her parents have agreed that we'll have the service at Sawmill Creek right near the water's edge. The reception will be in the lodge."

"Oh," said Davis, "that's just around the corner. So nobody is going to balk about not being in a church?"

"No, being on the water is more important for Megan and her folks than a particular building. She has an uncle who's a Deacon who is going to get permission to do a blessing, so there's no problem. Of course, we'd want you and your wife to be our guests."

Davis had the feeling that this would be a good experience, and that he and Beth would both enjoy the day when it came. After agreeing, he set the date on the calendar and got Megan's email address so that he could get the information that he'd need for his records.

"Now I owe you," said Wilson.

"What goes around comes around. Give Megan our best."

"And Beth as well."

Chapter 8

Lamb Weather

March near the shores of the Lake Erie is its own separate season which apparently has the option to be winter or spring. A major determinant is ice. If the lake is frozen, then the seasonal calendar may run directly from winter into summer. Forty-five degree days twenty miles away will hover around freezing when the wind is out of the north and super-chilled by the ice pack. The uninitiated turn their backs to this fact, but the locals understand its sweet rewards.

The benefits begin in the autumn when the 127.7 trillion gallons of water between the United States and Canada become a storage medium for heat that tempers the chill at night and holds back the frost. Of course when the jet stream brings the really frigid air, the warmer waters pack in the moisture that dumps early snow east of Cleveland and across northern Pennsylvania and New York. The counties west of Cleveland, however, avoid the worst of the lake effect snow.

Of course, the opposite holds true in the so-called spring. When the lake is frozen so is the land around it. As the weather warms and daylight lengthens, all the buds on trees to the south open. The immediate lakeshore, however, stays gripped in winter until the ice breaks. This postponement of spring is a blessing celebrated in orchards and vineyards whose fear is early blossoms and a late frost. The thaw delays the warm temperatures and the budding, merely a short-lived curse for the warmer-blooded whose recompense takes the form of apples, peaches, pears, grapes, and a land dotted with wineries open year round.

This particular year was a bit distressing. The lake had never had much of an ice blessing and the melt-off was complete by mid-March. Growers were sleeping uneasily. On the other hand, students at Firelands College were gathering in clusters outside rather than rushing into the buildings and classrooms any earlier than necessary.

Davis had just finished his Friday lecture and was walking toward the faculty lot when he heard his name.

"Dr. McGowan!" It was Ashley carrying her black book satchel over one shoulder, a black over-sized purse on the other, and her black mug in her right hand.

"Ashley, what is it?"

"I was wondering if I could set up an appointment to talk with you," she said taking a quick sip from the mug. Judging by the way she quickly pulled it away from her lips, it must have recently refilled and too hot.

"Of course," said Davis. "When do you have a free period?"

"I don't have anything right now," she said. "I saw you walking across campus and thought that I would take a chance to talk."

"Take a *chance*? It's part of my job to meet with students. Do you want to talk about your paper?"

The back-row-Goth-girl went silent for a moment. "No," she confessed. "The paper is going fine; it's even kinda fun. It's just that the last time we talked, you wondered why I said that I wasn't supposed to fit in."

Davis remembered the conversation in the Pit and how his asking had instantly shut her down. She went on talking as if a pause might break her resolve.

"I wasn't ready to talk then, but if I don't tell you, someone else will."

This all sounded very cryptic to McGowan, but there was also an urgency that he sensed.

"Do you want to find a place to sit down?" he said referring to the lounge area in the Pit.

"No," she said. "I don't want to have any of them eavesdropping. Can we just walk a little? It's not that cold."

It's an odd thing that a sunny forty-eight degree day in March is so much warmer than a raining fifty-five degree day in October. The fact was that the flip-flop had returned as a part of the school uniform. Ashley was still an exception with her black combat boots.

"Do you want to drop your book bag somewhere?" he asked.

"No, it's not heavy," she said shrugging her shoulders. Davis wondered if she would be the type to complain if she were also carrying a hod of bricks. His briefcase was not particularly heavy, however, so he set aside the idea of a quick trip to the car to drop it off. As he switched it from his right to left hand, it struck him that he and she might be more alike, at least in temperament, than appearance dictated.

"How about the lake?" he said as a suggestion that they could walk the paved perimeter of McBride Arboretum, a small on-campus nature preserve named for the College's first dean.

"That would be fine," she said. While there were some students out on the benches, the temperatures were not so inviting that anyone was staying long enough to listen to someone else's conversation. Still, it was a long while before Carpenter spoke.

"My family moved here five years ago," she began, "to Winsted." McGowan did not recognize the name, but it was probably one imported from Connecticut like most of the city names in the Firelands region of Ohio. The area was called *the Firelands* because of events of the American Revolution when British troops burned out civilians in order to cut off supplies and manufacturing from colonial forces. As reparation for the burnings, in 1792 the Connecticut legislature awarded a half-million acres in the Northwest Territory to be set aside for those affected by the conflict. Though most of the victims were too old to take advantage of the land grants (the survey was not complete until 1808), events were memorialized in place names like Greenwich, Norwalk, New Haven, East Haven, Danbury, Ridgefield, Groton, New London, and Fairfield.

"Winsted is just a small place," she added. "My brother was three years older than me. I was still in middle school, but when we came here, it was toward the end of his junior year."

"Where did you move from?" asked Davis, who quickly regretted changing the direction of her thought. *Just let her talk*, he admonished himself.

"We came from Knoxville, Tennessee," she said not hesitating. "Or near Knoxville. Brandon, that was my brother's name, was a big football star at Farragut High, and it was a real shocker to come to a small place like this."

McGowan listened intently and had heard the *was* when she had mentioned Brandon's name.

"The football coach had heard that Brandon was an all-state, all-conference quarterback in Tennesee and had a long talk with Brandon about playing for the Quarrymen his senior year." Davis presumed that the unusual word must have been the team name for whatever high school served Winsted, but he didn't ask for clarification.

"That's when the trouble started."

At this McGowan must have raised an eyebrow, because Ashley went immediately into an explanation.

"The guys who had been on the team all through high school were waiting for their senior year. It was supposed to be a good team, but, face it, Winsted had never been to even the District finals in football. But the quarterback and all the guys were pretty full of themselves. They thought this was the year.

"When Coach even started to talk about playoffs, they got excited until Brandon's name came up. It was against the rules, but he set up an off-season practice where he had his key players suit-up and scrimmage. Evidently Brandon blew them away with his ball handling and passing."

"You sound like you know a lot about the game," observed Davis who could sense her rising tension.

"It was a big part of our family," she said. "My dad was so pissed that the coach had broken the law by having a practice, but the damage was done."

"Somebody reported it?"

"You'd think that would have been the problem, but no. Coach had this Code of Secret that he drilled into them. Anybody broke on this and the season would be forfeited and there'd be no glory and no scholarships. My brother didn't care about any glory, but this was his way to go to college. My dad works for the railroad, and he does okay, but we aren't rich. Brandon wanted to go back to UT, but it would be out-of-state."

"Unless he was on a football scholarship," added Davis who made the quick leap from the Ohio's *UT* in nearby Toledo to the University of Tennessee.

"Exactly," she agreed. "No one said anything about what they did, but they hated Brandon; made his life miserable. Even during the practice, they would pull blocks to let him get clobbered."

"And the coach didn't notice?"

"He liked it! Especially when he'd get the passes off before he got hit. The ball kept bouncing off the helmet or back of the receivers and he'd yell, 'Turn around sooner, Damn it!'"

"Did your brother tell you all this?"

Ashley hesitated. "No, I saw it. I knew where they were meeting and I went with Brandon. Kept low in the car until everyone was too busy on the field to see me peeking over the dashboard."

Now it was Davis' turn to go silent. The conversation could go any direction, and he wasn't sure what to ask, if anything at all. He didn't have to.

"At the end, and I remember this so clearly, the coach had his arm around Brandon and was telling the *boys*, that was his word, that they had all summer to become *men*. He was going to coach a *man's team* in the fall, and they'd better get their butts in gear."

"No wonder they hated him," Davis said with a low whistle. "What did your brother do?"

"My brother was a man," she said as a tear began to wash away her eyeliner. "He offered to work out with them in the off-season. He could swallow his pride. He knew that it would take the entire team to get him what he wanted."

"An athletic scholarship to UT," said McGowan.

"That's what he wanted," she agreed.

"But...?" asked Davis when the pause went longer than expected.

"But they didn't see it that way," she said. "If he wanted to play football, they said, he should just go back to Rocky Top.

"After that he just sort of went into himself. He did a lot of exercise to keep himself in shape. He rode his bike all over Huron and Erie Counties."

"That's a pretty large area," noted McGowan.

"He was quite a cyclist, knew every bike trail and country road in two counties. He'd come home at night and tell me what he saw along the lake. It wasn't unusual for him to ride fifty or sixty miles. There was a stretch along the old Milan Canal that he liked. Over time he made friends along the way. I think that's what helped him endure the taunts of the other players. He'd just take off on his bike, hook up with a friend from another school, and spend some time fishing or boating. If the coach asked him if he was keeping up with his endurance training, he'd just say that he was doing road workouts on his bike and it was true."

"What happened when school started, and the team took to the field?" asked Davis. Ashley stopped walking and looked away toward a gathering of Canada geese that were making sure a grassy bank was properly littered with their green pellets. McGowan sensed that she might have been trying to frame the correct words, but when she spoke, he knew that she was rallying her vocal chords so that her voice would not betray her.

"He never went back his senior year," she said in a choking whisper.

"What?" asked McGowan, "Did he drop out?"

"No," she said, "He left. At least that's what everybody says. I don't believe it. He wouldn't leave without saying goodbye or making contact. We were a close family; he wouldn't just run away, and he wouldn't have murdered anyone."

The turn in the conversation confused Davis. "Murdered someone?"

"It's hard for me to understand, but the people who believe that it's true have thrown it at me so much that I can recite it in my sleep.

"I told you that he met people when he rode. He met this one guy; Aaron was his name. Brandon said he had gone to our school, but moved away soon after we came to town. I never knew his last name. When I first heard of him, he lived in Milan, somewhere near the bike trail.

"Aaron was sort of a loner, at least that's how Brandon put it. He wasn't much interested in sports, but he liked fishing and boating and reading–he read a lot–a really smart kid and they became pretty close. It was really kinda funny, my brother seemed like the major jock, but he really was more of a student, had more in common with Aaron than his teammates."

"What happened?" asked McGowan.

"The way they tell it, Brandon killed Aaron when they were fishing together one night out on the spoil area off Huron. It's just stupid to think about. I remember the police coming to our house. All they said was that something had happened and did we know where Brandon was.

"My folks didn't know exactly; they thought he was out on one of his cycling tours. He'd often come back after dark, and my Dad would get on his case about being on the roads at night. They figured that he must have got hit or something.

"I knew that he was planning to meet Aaron that night and they were going to fish for awhile either from the shore or use a canoe. Aaron's grandparents live about a block from the lake and had a canoe on some sort of wheeled dolly–I never saw it, but Brandon said it was pretty slick. Aaron could just wheel it down on the beach and slide it off with the fishing gear and everything. Brandon would hide his bike in the grass in the field near the water, and Aaron would paddle out to pick him up at the point.

"After I told them that, they sprung the news that Aaron had been killed. His skull was fractured by a cement block tied to a rope that looked like it was used as an anchor. They figured that someone must have got it swinging pretty hard to do as much damage as it did–someone pretty strong–and did we know where Brandon was.

"I said, 'He rode his bike,'" but they hadn't found any bike.

"I told them that he would hide it in the tall grass when they were going to use the canoe. They just looked at each other because they hadn't found any canoe either. I just assumed that when they talked about the cement anchor that they had found it in the canoe. A couple of days later, they found both."

It was an odd place for a story to end, but for a long while it seemed to Davis that Carpenter would not or could not go any further.

"There was a pretty heavy windstorm at the end of the month," she said at last. "A canoe washed up in Sheldon Marsh. It was easy enough for them to identify; it had the O-H numbers of the registration and they ran lab tests and found…" Again she paused as if the words hurt her mouth to speak… "blood and brain tissue. I wouldn't have thought that any of that would have been there after a few days in the water, but they have ways…"

"Did they find the bike?" asked Davis.

"Yes," she said. "It was south of Norwalk, down towards Olena. They said that he probably rode south and hitched a ride somewhere. They looked for him in Tennessee for a long time, figured that's where he'd head if he wanted to hide."

"Or maybe somebody dumped his bike," offered McGowan.

"That's what I said. I told them that my brother was not a murderer; he was just missing. His friend was killed and he was *missing*! But then I got a note."

Davis' surprised look became his question.

"A postcard came to me," she said. "It had a picture of Lake Hope on one side and on the side where you write, it was glued with cut-out words like the ransom notes in those old cheesy movies."

"What did it say?" asked McGowan.

"Just a few words: *Sis, I'm okay*, that's all. Didn't say who it was from or anything else, just *Sis, I'm okay*."

"And you don't think he was okay, do you?"

"He didn't do the damn note," she said.

"How do you know?"

"Two reasons. First, they already suspected that he went to Tennessee, and I think he could have gone there, but that Lake Hope is somewhere in southeast Ohio. That's not on any straight path to Tennessee. *But he's moving south, and in the right direction*, they said. That was true, but who would he know there?"

"You said there were two reasons," observed Davis.

"There were, but they didn't believe that either. He would *never* have called me *sis*. It's one of our word games. *Sis* was short for *sissy*, and neither of us was. He'd use another name if he wanted me to know it was him."

"What name would he have used?" asked Davis.

Ashley looked directly at McGowan as if to size him up for the first time, and then she spoke.

"*Katniss*," she said.

The reference was off the radar of most people in his generation, but he recognized it. Katniss Everdeen was the unstoppable hero of *The Hunger Games* series.

"No sissy!" said Davis.

"No, I'm not," she said. "When the evil stepsisters ask me if I've heard from my brother lately, I want to punch their faces, but I'm too strong to let them get to me. I have not heard from my brother since he rode off that day to go on an outing with a friend. He didn't kill his friend, and he didn't send me any sissy card."

"What do you think happened to him? asked McGowan.

"He's dead," she said with the sudden return of her Goth indifference.

Chapter 9

CPL

Beth was pleased when Davis told her that he would be meeting Darnell Wilson and Megan Sorento at Old First Church on Cleveland's Public Square. For the year prior to their African trip, Davis had broken his retirement in order to be the interim pastor of the historic congregation. As much as she was uneasy at his acceptance of the position when he first considered it, now that it was over, she missed their Wednesday forays into the city where his day in the office became her day at the CPL, Cleveland Public Library. She had spent the year working on the background material for a historical romance novel that wove its plot around local families caught up in the ill-fated presidency of Garfield. During her work, she had developed a number of friendships with the library staff, and with Colleen McQuisten at Old First.

The fact that Davis could commandeer some space for a counseling session spoke well of the fact that, even after the arrival of his successor, the congregation viewed his ongoing friendship as a plus. Of course, Megan and Darnell were not members and the wedding itself was to take place forty miles west in the sleepy little city of Huron. Old First was simply a convenient location to work around the convoluted schedules of an FBI agent and a Lakewood Detective.

Beth had already heard a secondhand account of the story that Ashley Carpenter had told about her brother and the violent death of Aaron Fahrenhauser some three or four years earlier.

Aaron had lived in Milan, a small town that found its place in history compliments of the birth of Thomas Alva Edison. That, and the annual Melon Festival, seemed to be among its greatest claims to fame. Brandon lived further out in the small crossroad's cluster of homes known as Winsted.

The librarians at CPL were surprised when she replaced her normal fare of historical research for one that went back four years and into the archives of the *Plain Dealer* and the much smaller *Norwalk Reflector*. They had all heard of the case, and each recounted sound bites from the television media coverage. They remembered seeing a picture of a clean-cut kid in a football jersey and hearing the unlikely admonition to contact the Erie County Sheriff's office if he was sighted in the area.

After several hours with the microfilm reader, Beth managed to scavenge newspaper reports of sightings in southern Ohio, Dallas, Texas, and Ogden, Utah. In every case, the evidence from surveillance cameras and eyewitnesses proved false. In the end, there was only an abandoned bike and a brutally mangled skull. One amateur profiler predicted that Brandon had most likely committed suicide out of remorse, and his body would might possibly be discovered in a remote location. That rabbit trail, however, ended abruptly when the County Sheriff's spokesperson announced that a postcard had been mailed to his parents' home. Again, Brandon Carpenter was a murderer-on-the-run. This time, he had slipped into Canada after turning all eyes south by means of a simple postmark from near Athens, Ohio. After that, the trail grew very cold and most people were back to watching reality television.

When Beth met up with Davis later that afternoon, she was the one who had the story to tell. He listened, carefully trying to find loose connections between all the reported conjecture of the press and the somber telling that came from Ashley. It was clear that the facts ran parallel and the conclusions, as few as they were, had very little basis in fact.

"I recounted Ashley's story to Sorento and Wilson," he said when she had finished. "They knew of the case, but wouldn't hazard a guess, though they were not too hot on the fugitive scenario."

"Seems sketchy to me as well," said Beth. "What did they think of the postcard?"

"That was the oddest of all. Megan said that it would have been a very dumb thing for someone to do, especially considering his cleverness at avoiding every other form of detection."

"One of the articles said that it might have been a ruse from the beginning, something to make everybody look the wrong way," agreed Beth.

"Megan wouldn't be a fan of that," said Davis. "She thought someone else sent it. Just didn't fit. I told her what Ashley told me about the fact that the brief note referred to her as *Sis*."

"What did Megan say to that?"

"She asked if he had any enemies. I said, most of an entire football team. Then I remembered what Sergeant Bill used to say."

Beth smiled. Sergeant Bill was a retired police officer in Dayton who continued to moonlight as an agent for a bail bond company. He'd get a call that some young fellow hadn't shown up in court after posting bail. Bill would go out and pick them up. Both she and Davis knew his secret for his always coming back with the fugitive. Of course, after years of church suppers most people knew the bail bondsman's secret, but he regaled the stories so well that no one ever jumped to the punch line.

"You go back to their house," said Beth. "They're probably hiding in the basement."

"Exactly," agreed Davis. "Megan and Darnell didn't dispute it. In fact, she pointed out how tough it is to completely break away from everything that's familiar, go to a new place, and never look back. Takes a lot of cash, too."

"That's what Bill would say. They'd always be within two blocks of where they lived, or with a family member or a friend," said Beth.

"What I didn't expect," said Davis, "was what Darnell said after that. They agreed that it was inconceivable that an eighteen-year-old, with no money, and not even a change of clothes could disappear, at least not without help. Then Megan got real quiet, and there was a lot of body language going on between the two of them. All the invisible-language conversation made me think that they'll do well together. They seem really good with each other.

"Anyway, she seemed to nod that it was okay and Darnell told me that she had an older brother who was killed back when she was in high school. I suppose that's one of the reasons she seemed so aware of the case, even though it happened some years ago in another jurisdiction, or at least the FBI wasn't called in."

"She had a brother killed?"

"That one was never solved, either," added McGowan. "Wilson didn't really go into details. Just made me respect the two of them even more."

"Bet it shutdown your premarital counseling session."

"Fortunately we were about done, but she's pretty tough. They both are. I suspect that they don't hide from many things. It's because of her brother that they want to be married near Lake Erie. Evidently, he was a sailor–used to crew Wednesday night races. That's when the mood lightened again. Darnell said that she promised him that she'd take him sailing sometime."

"Did you tell them that we have a boat?" asked Beth.

"Actually," said Davis, "they asked when we were going to be in the water, and whether our final session before the June wedding could be aboard a boat."

"And you said…"

"I think that you and I have been married long enough that you already know the answer to that."

"So will it be May or early June that we take them out?"

"We agreed to watch for a good weather window."

Chapter 10

Early Spring

It always makes the growers nervous when the fruit trees bud too early. This year, however, the cool spring nights did not carry any freeze that would nip grapes off the vine or destroy the promise of a good peach harvest.

For sailors, the itch to get on the water drove the marina operators crazy. Docks released from their moorings and tied off closer to shore for winter storage had to be floated back to their seasonal positions, and customers penned their optimistic best guesses for launch dates. Davis and Beth were no exception. Their daily walks now took them often through the forest of masts and hulls that crowded together in the marina parking lot.

Sailors refer to this blacktop storage as *sitting on the hard*, and this necessary evil provided the opportunity to inspect and repair the underside of the hull and renew the antifouling paint that was meant to keep off the algae and, in the case of Lake Erie, the zebra mussels that had invaded the Great Lakes.

Golden Willow was nested between two much larger vessels. The name was a carry-over from the previous owners who recognized that its gold anodized aluminum mast and spars were distinctly different than the usual silver, white, or black of most rigs. The McGowans kept the name because it seemed appropriate rather than out of respect for the old sailor's superstition that boats react badly to being renamed.

Their friends had suggested a great many names. *Parsonage* was a popular choice, but Davis would have no part of it. This was his escape, not an extension of his career. Of course that led to a second choice: *Why not call it Escape?* This became the next of the renamers' mantras. Of course that name was already a worn out cliché to every veteran mariner.

In the end, the truth emerged. No one hated *Golden Willow*, they just wanted an excuse to party. The renaming ritual is fairly well defined and requires several bottles of champagne. The first bottle must be exhausted by toasts and tributes to the old name. A second is poured over the bow when the new name is proclaimed. Of course, this is then followed by toasts and best wishes for the newly inaugurated craft.

"How about we just keep the old name," said Davis, "and just have a welcome aboard party?" With that the renaming pressure had ended and the sea gods were not offended.

The no-offense plan was working. The bottom was still not showing any telltale cracks that would require grinding and sealing before the new bottom paint could be added. Still, that was toxic work and Beth insisted that Davis wear protective coveralls when he crawled under the hull to apply the thick biocide with a brush and a spattering roller. It was not the most fun part of the sport of sailing, but it was an annual ritual observed by all with the strength to do it, and thus, avoid the expense of having it done professionally.

Beth found an excuse to be busy the morning that Davis masked off the waterline and began to stir up the tar that had settled to the bottom of the paint can. His reverie was interrupted before it had gotten very far.

"Davis," said a pair of jeans that were moving through the maze of parked boats. He assumed there was an upper body attached to the pants, but the paint fumes may have been playing tricks.

"Over here," he called. Ryan Richardson soon appeared from behind an oversized rudder.

"There you are," he said. "I called the house and Beth said you were over here."

"Working on your boat, too?" jibed McGowan. Richardson was a fellow board member at the condo association where he and Beth first lived when they moved to Huron. Early on, Ryan tried to convince them that they should join the yacht club. *Do you have a boat?* Davis had asked at the time. That was when he learned that many of the club members did not have boats. Instead, they had raffles, parties, and cookouts. The McGowans resisted the initiation fee and chose to sit peacefully in the cockpit of *Golden Willow* while the sunlight faded on the old grain elevators across the river.

"What do you need, Ryan?"

"We had a big problem this winter," began Richardson. "A big problem. We lost a lot of water from the swimming pool."

The image took Davis by surprise. The Association had had a new liner installed a few years earlier when he was serving as its treasurer. "That's not good!" he said.

"Tell me about it," agreed Ryan. "With all the money we spent."

Davis remembered the debate when the twenty-five year old vinyl liner had failed before. After much discussion, the board bit the proverbial bullet and did the project *right* with new water lines and concrete decking. "Shouldn't it still be under warranty?" he asked.

"We thought so," said Richardson. "We called the pool company and they hemmed and hawed saying that it wasn't possible."

"Neither is heavier than air flight," said Davis.

"Exactly! I said that if it was so impossible how come there's only water in the deep end. They said that they'd be out in a few weeks, but we must have done something wrong."

"Nice," said McGowan.

"Anyway, you were the treasurer when the new pool was put in and we were wondering if you might have any of the documentation."

Davis thought about it for a moment. He always entered the data in the accounting software and stuffed the actual receipts in an envelope. When he handed over the materials to the new treasurer, all she wanted was the *neatified* version of the computer printouts. He was sure that he had not thrown away any records, but now they must live in one of the unopened storage boxes in his garage.

"I might have them," was his most definitive response. "I'll have to check."

"Fair enough," said the always affable Richardson.

"When do you need them? I'll have to do some digging."

"Doesn't sound like they're in any big hurry to come out and check it. Guess they're going to get as many pools open as they can before they tackle any other maintenance projects."

"Spring is coming on pretty quickly," said Davis. "Want to stay and help me put this stuff on," he said pointing to the paint can.

"Are you kidding! I'm not into all that boat crap! That's why I belong to the yacht club!"

Chapter 11

Saturday Night

Ministers' wives are generally expected to conform to a dress code that falls in one or more of the following descriptive categories: dull, dumpy, boring, modest, or unappealing. Davis always supposed that it went with a general cultural fear of human sexuality. He remembered his early years in the ministry when one elderly parishioner made a disparaging comment about his predecessor. "They have five children," was the actual quote that was delivered with disdain. Obviously, she felt that there was just too much sexual activity in the marriage. He wondered what she would think if she actually opened her Bible to read the *Song of Solomon* or the proverb that read:

> Three things are too wonderful for me;
> four I do not understand:
> the way of an eagle in the sky,
> the way of a serpent on a rock,
> the way of a ship on the sea,
> and the way of a man and a woman.
> *(Pv 30:18,19)*

McGowan wondered if the old biddy had any choice words for Beth who was well proportioned and attractive. Of course, she gave in to the downgraded wardrobe pressure of public opinion. Ministers' wives were to dress like dumplings, and Davis savored times away when they could dress like two people in love and approaching the margins of provocative.

Beth had once taken an *Are you sexy enough?* quiz featured in one of the women's magazines at the hair salon. It required ranking yourself in various categories. *Good looking with effort* had been her choice on the attractiveness scale. Davis would have more likely rated her *Where's the modeling contract?* instead. He thought her stunning and if she needed a little effort to look good, it was entirely a wardrobe update and a setting aside of the now ingrained idea of how she was supposed to look. When she ditched the preacher-wife rags, she was clearly stunning, even as she approached sixty.

There were live bands at Sawmill Creek on Saturday nights, and the two enjoyed both the dancing and each other's company. In time, Beth noticed that they did get looks from people seated around the tables near the dance floor, but they held no disdain. On the slow dances, they could wrap arms around each other and sway.

"People are looking at us," she once noted.

"And what do they see?" he asked. She had no real comeback, so he filled in the blank. "They see a hot woman and an old man who's crazy about her."

Beth laughed, maybe at the outrageousness or the truth of it. "They see two people in love," she retorted.

"I'll buy that."

The fact was that Saturday nights brought out all sorts of people. There were the regulars who gathered as couples or clusters of friends or loners looking to find a way to not be alone. Then there were the dancing stars. These were not necessarily the couples who had taken lessons or danced with each other for so many years that moved with an easy grace of knowing every next movement of their partner. The *stars*, however, looked quite different. They needed a partner in the way a comic needed a straight man. The purpose of the one was to accentuate the other. Arms flourished. Legs extended and the uninitiated who ventured into the zone would find themselves jostled, bumped, or poked with a characteristic, *Sorry!*

Davis wondered what they were sorry about. Were the newly battered amateurs simply paying the price for obstructing the grandeur of the dance? Many times the stars were visiting dance instructors. After several rounds of the ballroom version of *Saturday Night Fever*, patrons would find business cards placed on the tables near the melting ice in their drink glasses.

The marketing strategy definitely worked. The proof was that on some evenings a graduating class would arrive in full academic regalia which, in this case, meant the correct shoes that were slipped on at the tables in anticipation of that moment when they were beckoned to the floor.

Fortunately for the *non-stars* like the McGowans, the students didn't take on the more violent attributes of their teachers. They had taken the class to correct a lingering *two-left-feet syndrome*, or to rejuvenate, inaugurate, or captivate a partner who would make Saturday night into a pattern of intimacy.

The really good bands brought out the disciples of dance who followed the groups that fit their style or promoted their particular brand. *Kruze* was such a band, and Davis was glad to see them listed on the marquee when they pulled into the lot nearest the lodge.

It must have been graduation night. Several men had already shod themselves with black and white wing-tips, *ballroom modern*, to be precise. One in particular stood out to Davis. The gray-haired man was probably in his mid to late sixties and had a matching moustache. In addition to the shoes that showed off his footwork, he wore a shiny belt buckle medallion around his waist. Otherwise, everything else, pants, shirt, belt strap, was jet-black. He was dressed to impress, and it didn't take a Sherlock to figure it out. His partner was an attractive woman ten to fifteen years his junior. He held out his hand as he escorted her toward the dance. He seemed mesmerized, and she radiant. McGowan thought that, though the dance lessons informed their method, and their quick-stepping feet flashed white and silver, the real style was the *something else between them*.

It all came to an abrupt halt, however, when he slid to the floor and there was a collective gasp that stopped everything. Cell phones were withdrawn and the 911 operator was suddenly inundated.

The security guard rushed to bring out a defibrillator and his companion struggled to slip a nitro tablet through his clenched jaws. The squad arrived in time to take over the CPR duties that had already started. Everything was quick and efficient. IV drip, shirt ripped open, pads applied upper right and lower left, the order to clear, the click, stop, listen, clear, click, stop, listen, clear, the gurney, the transfer lift, and finally, the littered empty floor.

The band announced a break while the room tried to recover its breath. Unfortunately, the music in the queue was their usual number, and *The Electric Slide* took on a bizarre twist. The evening had ended.

Davis had seen death many times before. He had been in hospital rooms when life had gone. Sometimes he had been called to the bedsides of the newly deceased and prayed with families over cooling flesh. After the funeral, his practice was to stay behind when the casket was sealed. There had been times when the family needed to know that someone was there, that the job was done correctly, and that in the end there was respect. It was a small thing done hundreds of times. How many funerals had he conducted? Close to a thousand was his rough calculation.

The man on the dance floor, however, was different. Though he was a stranger, they were brothers bound through dance and the love of a partner. McGowan did not know the man's condition, but he had seen enough to suspect that a life had closed in the midst of itself.

Chapter 12

Knockdown

Golden Willow was off the hard before the end of April, and the weather was still hinting at an early summer. Lake temperature was already into the high sixties, evidence of unusually hot days and nights that stayed in the fifties. At the dock, Beth and Davis fulfilled all the springtime rituals to awaken the vessel after its winter hibernation.

In chilly damp weather, the oil changing, water tank cleaning, and scrubbing chores had to be followed by a retreat to a hot drink in a warm space. When the air temperature hits the mid-seventies, there are no disagreeable tasks, just outfitting a boat and a renewing a dream. The dreaming was amplified further by the fact that that same day, the bay at the mouth of the Huron River was alive with sails shaking out the folds of their winter exile.

For all the activity in the water, there was only one gold mast, and the perfect day brought the idea of sailing west to the islands. When he was a graduate student at Princeton, Davis learned that people from Jersey went to the shore. In California, they followed the surf, and on Lake Erie, the western islands are the Christopher Cross equivalent to paradise. In the summer, the bands at local clubs generally marketed this with Hawaiian shirts and a full range of Jimmy Buffett songs. This was Ohio's Vacationland, and out-of-state license plates underscored the theme. Activity along the north coast created traffic jams and increased demand for passage on one of the ferries crossing over to Kelley's Island or Put-in-Bay on South Bass Island.

Beth suggested an early season excursion to Middle Bass Island. It was more removed from the party atmosphere of the Bay that rocked all summer, and within its quiet environs was a nature preserve that provided an escape.

"Friday after I get back from class," said Davis.

"What?" said Beth, who had not been privy to the first part of the conversation that was going on in McGowan's head.

"Why don't we take off for Middle Bass on Friday?" he said repeating his thought in the more complete form.

"Under one condition," his wife added.

"And that would be?"

"That the weather doesn't go all *Ohio spring* on us!"

"You mean, sixty-two and rainy. I can live with that."

So the day of departure was set and the weather anomaly that had transformed late April to early June continued. Friday was to be mid- to upper seventies with a 40% chance of late afternoon thunderstorms, which is the price to be paid for warm air over cool water.

"We should be okay," said Davis. "If we get off by 10:00 we should be tucked away on Middle Bass by 3:00." But a student needed to discuss a term paper, Beth ran out for a new can of sunscreen, and McGowan stopped at the marine store to pick up a spare impellor for the engine. "I should have already changed it," he said, "the one that's in there now is six years old." The result was a late start on a spring morning that promised a summer's day.

Golden Willow didn't seem perturbed by the delay; she seemed grateful to be back in the water and took to the ten knot winds by leaping to hull speed. The growing cloud bank on the western horizon looked like it held rain, but the foul weather gear was in the hanging locker if needed.

"The best-laid schemes o' mice and men," wrote Robert Burns, "Gang aft a-gley." Just off the western shore of Kelley's, this scheme went about as a-gley as it could. Ahead of them was an open passage that would take at least an hour, and Davis saw a lightning strike to the south over Marblehead. To the north a storm was brewing over Pelee Island on the Canadian side. Flashes in that direction said that there might be bumpy water ahead. Then again, the skies ahead were brighter and with any luck they could shoot the gap between two wicked cloud banks.

Beth was lounging on the foredeck when Davis felt the air grow suddenly cold.

"Beth, go below and get the foul weather gear."

"It's nice," she said unaware of the deterioration that was upon them. "The rain will feel good."

"Get the gear, now," said Captain Bly, and Beth wasn't sure about the sudden tone shift. She did go below and stopped to pick up a soda can that was left on the cockpit bench.

"Hurry," called Davis as a very cold rain began to fall.

"Why are you acting like this?" she said.

"Because I don't want hyperthermia. Move quickly." She was still miffed, at least until she came back out into the weather and experienced the twenty degree shift in temperature.

"What's happening?"

"Everything," he said as he eased the mainsail. "I should have reefed a long time ago."

"What? But it was nice," said Beth. "What do you want me to do?"

"But I saw those clouds." The waves had picked up and the foredeck was bucking with each hit. No one could go out there without being thrown from the boat. "Take the mainsheet," he ordered handing her the end of the line that controlled the angle of the mainsail to the wind. "Let it out when I tell you."

The boat was headed north on a beam reach when a microburst took hold and swung *Golden Willow* ninety degrees. The sudden shift rolled the boat over as she turned violently to the east.

"Let out the main–just let it go all the way," he commanded. He heard the line racing through the sheave and the boom swung violently carried by the wind. Still *Golden Willow* continued to roll onto its side. Davis reached for the jib sheet and let the sail blow free. The sails were flapping like banners in a hurricane, the noise was deafening, and the rain was stinging.

"Show your stuff," he said to the boat. "You're supposed to right yourself." The ocean-capable craft had high combings, but water was beginning to spill into the cockpit. McGowan's eyes flitted to the open companionway. If water reached that with any force, they'd sink in seconds.

"Come on, *Willow*." It was one of those slow-motion moments. He held his breath and tried to will the laws of physics to take over and let the iron keel pull the boat back to upright. He looked in the direction that they were headed, the course he had not chosen. They were racing toward the rocky riprap on the southwest corner of the island. "We're going to run aground," he said and suddenly felt like he was talking to himself. He reached for the ignition and the diesel engine fired quickly. "Stay in the boat," he said turning to look back, but Beth was not there. "Keep in the boat," he said again turning further and being relieved to see that, though she had been thrown across the cockpit, she was not in the water.

Golden Willow remembered its deep-water pedigree and began to right itself. The propeller gripped the water and the wheel began to respond. Davis could count the stones on the breakers and hoped against hope that there was enough water under the keel to keep the fiberglass afloat now that he could turn it into the wind and fight against the oncoming surge in the struggle to crawl off the shoreline.

Later, he would learn that the winds had hit fifty-five knots, but what he knew now was that the twenty-four horsepower that throbbed below the deck was not enough to fight the force of the storm. The engine was at full throttle. The bow was into the wind, and slowly Erie was winning. They were still being pushed backwards. He suddenly thought of a man on the dance floor facing an ending that had never been anticipated when the evening began.

Instinctively he grabbed the flapping rope that was tied to the end of the boom. He pulled. He pulled hard and drew the boom toward the center of the boat. When it was nearly over his head, the wind caught the mainsail, and *Willow* started to sail forward.

He did everything wrong. He wrapped the line around his hand. He had to since there was no cleat to grip it. A broken hand or arm was less dangerous than the rocks, but neither was to be his fate.

Golden Willow crawled until it outlasted the wind and the wall of rain that made them lose sight of everything except what could have been a limestone monument to the futility of humans over nature.

They were alive in a cold drizzle. The seas had settled and the Volvo marine engine took control of their course. Beth may have been in shock. She was definitely bruised, but she took the wheel as Davis went up atop to take down the sails. The jib lines looked like tightly knotted spaghetti, but he lashed the sail to the deck. Then he dropped the main and used shock chords to secure it to the boom.

"Nice sail, huh?" he said as he took the wheel back from Beth.

"I never thought it would get this cold," she said. The fact was that they were relatively dry beneath their jackets, but wet hair and legs suggested something different.

"The bad news," began Davis, "is that the front hatch blew open and we must have five gallons of water in our bunk." The visibility was much better now, though the rain looked like it would stay for quite a while. They were still an hour-and-a-half from Middle Bass, but only half-an-hour from the breakwall that protected the marinas on Kelley's. "I say that we dock here tonight."

She did not argue. At McGowan's insistence, they ate a couple of granola bars. "We need the calories," he said.

They both felt better, however, when the dock lines were tied off and they were snugged securely in a berth. The rain had stopped and the breeze presented the possibility of drying out some very wet bedding.

Davis went to the marina office to register and pay the fees while Beth separated the *could-be-dried* linens from the *no-way* fabrics and pillows. When he returned he was wearing a silly grin.

"Do I look that funny?" she asked.

"No," he said, "you look remarkably alive! It's just that when I registered, they gave me this wooden token for five dollars off at the restaurant. Then they told me that almost everyone took off on the ferry before the storm hit and they sent their staff home."

"So we have a wooden nickel with no place to use it."

"That's about it. Do you feel like taking a walk into town? I think we've earned it."

She put up no argument, and they secured what they needed to and clothespinned the sheets and blankets to the lifelines. The sky was clear again and the sunny day had returned.

Two marinas over, the kitchens were still open. Beth and Davis ordered burgers and toasted their miraculous rebirth with a margarita and a Glenlivet, straight up. Other storm survivors began to gather. Most, however, were power boaters who made harbor before the fury, or tourists who were waiting for calmer seas before returning to the mainland ports of Catawba or Port Clinton.

The McGowans had survived the chaos of the storm. Beth attributed it to sailing skill. Davis was not so sure that it wasn't dumb luck and a solid boat. "Here's to *Golden Willow*," he said raising a glass.

"Did you get caught in that?" asked a woman seated with a family across the aisle.

"Sure did," said Davis, "and suddenly life seems very good."

Halfway through the retelling, McGowan realized that he was obviously beginning to debrief a trauma. This had been more than a story. Beth found her voice as well and recounted her anger when Davis had been so demanding, and pledged her allegiance in the future.

When the food arrived, McGowan's energy began to subside. He asked where the strangers had come from and whether they were boaters. They had come across on the ferry and were looking forward to better weather for the remainder of the weekend. They were staying in a B&B and were renting several golf carts to explore the island.

"Where are you from?" asked Davis.

"We live southeast of Norwalk," said the stranger, "in a little crossroads called Winsted. Bet you never heard of it."

"Actually," began McGowan, "one of my students is from there. *Carpenter* is her family name."

The man looked blank until his wife added, "That's the family with the girl who always wears black."

"That's her," said Davis, "a bright kid."

The man nodded his *aha* at the mention of Ashley's wardrobe statement, but offered no further elaboration.

"We only moved there a year ago," he said almost apologetically. "I don't think there are many secrets in that place, but we're the newcomers and don't get told too much."

Davis hesitated and then pushed the topic. "Ashley's older brother was evidently going to be the quarterback on the football team a few years ago."

"Quarterback? I can't imagine that the high school would have two from tiny little Winsted. We bought our house from the family whose son was the quarterback. It was real sad. He had been a local star, and went to Ohio University, but got cut from the team. He came back to Winsted, but…"

"It was one of those teen things that you read in the newspaper," continued his wife. "He must have been drinking and drove off the road one night. High speed thing. Hit a ridge in the road and went airborne. From what we heard, it pretty much broke up the family. Parents split. We kinda felt bad about buying their house, but they were in a tight place and were already moving on. Sad story."

"That is sad," said Davis. "I must have misunderstood what Ashley told me earlier."

By the time that darkness claimed the marina, the bunk had dried significantly. Most of the water had settled in the mattress topper, and that was stripped and moved to the main cabin. In the morning they headed for home. The winds were very light, and they motored for the first hour. McGowan didn't mind. In fact, he held his Volvo in new respect. Still, when the wind began to liven, they replaced the diesel with white sails which were controlled by the old lines newly untangled.

They were docked at their marina on the Huron River, and the sails were all stowed when Beth pointed at the clouds mounting in the southwest.

"It's happening again," said Davis.

They were seated in their own living room when this new storm hit with the intensity of the day before.

"Make a note," said Davis, "I'm not in favor of spring thunderstorms."

"That makes two of us," said Beth.

Chapter 13

Dumpster Diving

Davis had not forgotten his promise to Ryan and found himself out in his garage looking through all the old boxes of stuff that didn't need to be kept, but shouldn't have been actually thrown away. He and Beth thought of them as prepackaged dumpster fare that their heirs could toss out directly when they died, or worse, became feeble of mind. *If it's still out here after three years, we probably didn't need it,* was his usual reply to the question: *What's in all those boxes?* As he now ruffled through the contents of a few, his logic was coming into question.

Among the junk items were toys from children who had left home years earlier. These little bits might just hold more value than the signed prints on the living room walls. Then there was the fact that some of these held the corporate memory of small organizations like the Lexington Glen Condo Association.

When he and Beth sold their condo and moved into a fixer-upper nearer the lake, he had transferred all his records on a CD that he had burned. The new treasurer, however, saw no need to keep all the receipts and scraps of paper that were already summarized and filed so neatly as line items on a financial statement. Now one of those scraps was needed or could be needed if a ten-year product had failed in less than five, and the installer had amnesia about the product details.

Davis knew exactly what they wanted. They wanted a tri-fold brochure from the Paradise Pool Company. The sales representative had underlined the words *ten year liner guarantee* in the descriptive paragraph under a tranquil image of swirling blue streaks sparkling under pristine water. McGowan was either blessed or cursed by the ability to remember extraneous things. He had never given much thought to it until someone pointed it out during the year he was at the College Hill Church in Dayton. He had inadvertently saved a meeting from a blow-up by recalling the details of an event that had taken place two months earlier. When both sides of the dispute agreed that his recollection was spot-on, they settled in to understanding the differing points of view. At the end, one disputant observed, *you have a photographic memory!*

He hadn't thought of it that way because he wasn't remembering something on a page. His brain, however, processed images and he could see the event as it happened. He knew who was sitting where and what they said and how they turned when a contradictory opinion was stated.

Maybe he did have eidetic memory, if it even existed, but the memory of that meeting was of an elderly grandmother who was there. She was tickled by the *photographic memory* comment and, forever after, teased Davis about having a *pornographic memory*.

"There's the fellow with the pornographic memory," she would say softly as he walked past at church suppers. She was a sweetheart as far as Davis was concerned. This African-American great-grandmother had had a life with troubles that he could barely imagine. Whenever he heard the tease, it reminded him to stop and laugh with her. Whatever he was rushing toward could not be more important than this gray-haired *Mother of the Church*. In Roman Catholic circles, such a title belonged to the Virgin Mary, but in the African-American churches it was often applied unofficially to particularly nurturing and prayerful elders. It was not a position that could be aspired to, it was one that emerged through character. She had it, and she was one.

"Here it is," said McGowan as he pulled the printed brochure from a jumble of bits and pieces in a shoebox. There was the pamphlet as he remembered. Stapled to it was the bill describing the work done and the SKU number of the liner. The eureka moment was tempered by the necessity to repack the pieces of the chaos created by the search. He applied as much thought to that as he had to the original dumping. *Here's something else for the kids to figure out*, he thought.

Even though the condos were less than a half mile away, the trip over to them was a journey back in time. Lexington Glen was located just off a well-traveled road, but not one the McGowan's used since their move. The road looped around the high school and the athletic field. On football night, the streets were parked solid, and Monday through Friday, there was a sort of rush hour that marked the opening and closing of school. Today Davis beat the school traffic. With no cars in his rearview mirror, he reverted to his habit of looking over the guardrail before entering the turnoff into the Association property.

The thunderstorms that created so much havoc on the lake also delivered enough rain to saturate the county and flood all the tributaries that dumped into it. Washburn Ditch was one of those watercourses. In the horse-and-buggy days of the 1800's, it was probably a mostly dry creek bed that raced wildly in a spring torrent and then subsided to a few deep mud holes in August. Now, after a long sequence of road building and improvements, it was funneled through massive concrete pipes that went under the highway so that drivers were unaware that it was still there.

Condo residents knew. With the spring floods, the water would rise, and, though it never threatened any homes, it created a lake that turned a line of elms and willows into islands that might strand the squirrels that lived in the tangled woods on either side of the flow. The size of the lake was based both on the shape of the low-lying basin and on the tangles of debris that had been left from the year previous. The outlet for the water was only a quarter mile away where it passed under Cleveland Road and into Lake Erie. There never was any threat for flooding; even the Corps of Engineers agreed with that. Still, residents worried about tree roots being undercut by the flood, and for good reason. The softened ground encouraged the fat willows to roll in the direction of their leaning trunks. It would take them years, but one day the root ball would become unstuck and the tree would topple into the ditch after pulling a wall of dirt out of the ground forming a frog grotto.

"We need to clean out that creek," was the cry at every annual meeting. The fact was that the area was designated for wildlife and meant to be left untouched. The falling trees were never a danger to buildings or other property, but they did attract birds of every sort, and, for awhile at least, a red fox.

Today, the water was into the trees. Davis could see it clearly over the rail as he drove past, and then it was obscured by trees as he turned into the Association access road. The swimming pool was straight ahead of him, and he could see, even from a distance, that the water was way down below the concrete decking. He pulled into one of the spaces in front of the chain link fence that guarded the perimeter, picked up the brochure from the passenger seat and got out of the car.

Ryan Richardson must have seen him pull in and came out of a nearby condo to meet him.

"What a mess!" he said as he stepped in to share Davis' view.

"That's just not right," said McGowan. "If you have a problem with Paradise Pools, this should help." He handed over the brochure and the receipt to Richardson who brightened at the recognition.

"I think they were going to try and fight this," he said, "this should help."

"How could they fight it?" asked Davis. "The leak is obvious."

"Well they haven't really got in to look at it yet. They're having someone come out from the company that made the liner, but the guy that was here said we must have done something or some vandal stuck something down through the plastic. Here, I'll show you." He opened the padlock and they entered the pool area. Ryan pointed to a depression in the floor of the pool where the murky water that still lived in the deep end lapped and splashed into it. "See that?"

"What the?" asked McGowan. "There must be a hole there. It couldn't have been there last season. You would have known."

"And it wasn't there when it was covered last fall!" Davis remembered that the pool was always covered with a green mesh to prevent leaves from getting into the water in the off-season. "Hell," Ryan continued. "They were the ones who put the cover on when they winterized it. Actually, they were the ones who took it off when we told them about it. They said we had to because it was drooping so low that it would tear under its own weight.

"If someone threw something really heavy or sharp at it when it was covered there'd be a cut in the cover, wouldn't there?" suggested Davis.

"Exactly," agreed Richardson. "But there's no rip in the cover. Sounds like a manufacturer's defect to me!"

"Sounds like a pain in the butt to me," said McGowan. "Let me guess. You're getting phone calls like: *Hey, Ryan, the pool will still be open by Memorial Day, right?*"

"That, and *I think that tree down by the creek is going to fall, shouldn't you do something about it?* I'll bet you miss this place. Wanna come back?"

"I'm getting too old," said Davis, "the doctor says that I shouldn't try catching falling trees anymore."

"I haven't been feeling well myself," said Richardson, "maybe you could give me the name of that doctor."

Chapter 14

Person of Interest

When the phone rang, the caller ID indicated a number that Davis had never seen before. The name, however, was close to being familiar. It read *Matthew Fornesb*, which he took to be the abbreviation occasioned by the screen size on his wireless landline. He and Beth had dined with Matt's father and step-mother at JFK months earlier.

"Hello."

"Dr. McGowan, this is Matt Fornesby. How are you doing?"

"We're fine, Matt. Had a good visit with your father awhile back."

"He said that. Actually, that's why I'm calling."

"Is he alright?" Davis realized how conditioned he had become to having people call in times of crisis.

"He's fine. They're both fine," he said adding in a reference to Molly. "It's just that they're coming to Cleveland next week and I thought that if the weather holds like this, they might like to see a little bit of the countryside out where you live. Would you mind if we dropped in? Now that Dad's retiring, I think he's trying to reconnect with some of his non-work friends. If there's a nice restaurant, I'd be glad to take you all to dinner."

"Well, the places might not be quite up to your father's standards, but there are a few choices, but that's on one condition."

"What's that?"

"It'll be my treat. Your father took us out to dinner last time and threw in first-class seating as an extra. I think it's my turn."

There was a brief silence on the other end of the connection, and Davis expected that Matt was unsure of the twist in arrangements. Even though he was thirty years younger, he probably had more annual family income than the McGowans ever had.

"I guess," he said, with a *we'll see* quality in his voice. Davis didn't offer any protest. After all, he knew most of the servers and could manage a bit of subterfuge if it came to rerouting a check.

They spoke briefly and negotiated the date. As they were talking, however, the doorbell rang. Davis looked out the front window and saw a police cruiser parked at the end of his drive.

"I have to go now," said Davis, "there's a cop car in my driveway."

"What did you do now?" asked Matt, more like an old friend than a graduate of McGowan's high school youth group.

"Nothing that I know of," said Davis. He wondered if Matt remembered the day when the police came to his home. Of course he would. It was the day that his mother had died in an upstairs bedroom, and his family was changed forever. "Tell your Dad and Molly that we're looking forward to getting together with all four of you. Say 'hello' to Erin, too."

"And say 'hi' to Mrs. McGowan for me," and the generational wall was back.

Before he could offer a greeting to the officer standing on the front stoop, he heard his own name spoken.

"Davis McGowan?" said the policeman. His words started strongly but had an inflection at the end that implied doubt or surprise.

"Yes, what can I do for you?"

"I'm Sergeant Bostwick," said the thirty-something man with a stern expression. "I'd like to ask you a couple of questions, if I might."

"What about?" With this, the man looked at a small electronic tablet that he had been carrying in his right hand.

"I was talking to Ryan Richardson, and he said that you were in charge when the pool was rebuilt at Lexington Glen."

"Yes, I was. I knew that the pool liner got a leak over the winter, but I didn't realize that it would become a federal case." His attempt at humor did not lighten the expression on the sergeant's face, and McGowan would have liked to take the words back.

"May I come in?"

"Sure," said Davis who was more confused than ever. The officer removed his cap as he crossed the threshold, and McGowan indicated that he could take a seat on the sofa. He sat opposite on a matching overstuffed chair. "I don't understand the problem with the pool," he said.

Bostwick ignored the remark and proceeded to his own agenda. "Can you tell me what transpired during the time that the pool liner was installed?"

Davis was still confused. "You mean why the work had to be done and why we decided to redo the whole thing?"

"I'm more interested in construction aspects," said the sergeant. "I understand that you were the one who worked closely with the installation team on a day-to-day basis."

"Well, I usually looked over the fence to see what was going on–our condo was right next to the pool. The foreman of the work crew would sometimes double check to make sure I understood what they were doing."

"Did you understand?"

"Sure, it's pretty straight-forward stuff. I've always been a do-it-yourselfer and I actually worked for a pool company when I was in grad school." This last comment had the officer enter something quickly on his notepad.

"Was there anything they did that made you wonder?"

"Not particularly. Like I said, I had done this sort of thing before. I never actually installed a pool, but I'd helped repair broken lines and knew the mechanics of all the underground systems, the filters, skimmers, and stuff like that."

"Did anyone else know that?"

"I made small talk with the foreman when they started the demolition on the concrete. I suppose that's why he kept me informed about what was going on–he knew I'd understand."

"Now you're saying that he kept you informed."

"Well, when we talked," offered McGowan. "Has something happened?"

"You don't have to answer my questions now," said Bostwick. "I can set up a deposition where you could have an attorney."

"No," said Davis backing off quickly, "it's not that. I just don't know where you are heading. We had a liner dump a lot of water underground and had to have the pool redone. I tried to keep tabs on what was going on and I wrote the checks to pay the bills. I was the treasurer and the board member who lived next door. I suppose I was more curious than most because I had worked on pools. I didn't know much about underground liner pools, but I remembered being told how they were installed back in my Princeton days."

"I understand," said the officer, "I just don't want to say anything in advance that may jaundice your memory of events. This all must sound very petty, but what you're telling me helps."

Davis relaxed as Bostwick framed a new question.

"You said that the foreman–do you remember his name?–kept you informed. About what, specifically?"

"I don't remember his last name, but I think his first name was *Don*. The biggest thing I remember was that he wanted me to understand about the drain at the deep end."

"What about the drain?"

"Only that they weren't putting one in, but I was the one who brought up the subject when we asked for a bid. It just made things simpler."

"How so?"

"I knew that the regulations changed from the time our pool was originally installed in the seventies. The vacuum force created at the deep end had actually caused drownings. Kids who didn't weigh much could be sucked to the bottom where they could be held with so much force that they couldn't swim away. The result was that drains had to be turned off or sealed. There was even a new regulation about adding some kind of retrofit device to cover even the sealed drains."

"So it wouldn't make much sense to put in a new liner with an illegal drain," said the sergeant.

"Exactly," agreed Davis. "The issue for us was that technically this wasn't a *new* pool; it was a repair. The sidewalls stayed in place, so we were just replacing a liner."

"Seems like there's not much difference," observed Bostwick.

"Actually, it meant thousands of dollars for the condo association."

"I don't get it."

"Regulations!" said Davis. "The pool is really private, but we get inspected like any public pool, even though the condo owners are the only ones allowed to use the pool. There are no special fees or memberships. Anyway, since the time the pool was originally installed, rules for public pools were being changed–in fact; I don't think you can have vinyl liners anymore if you are classified as a *public* pool. We had to be grandfathered and couldn't change anything considered substantial."

"So the drain not being replaced didn't count."

"That's the way we proposed it. The one that had been there had been shut off and sealed for years; we couldn't see much value in adding a fake drain to a replacement liner."

"That makes sense."

"So I got to see it done. It's actually pretty slick. They compact the soil on the bottom and trowel on a couple inches of sand. The liner is set out over the surface and they start adding water. The weight of the water presses evenly over the vinyl skin and they use something like a shop vac to suck out any air that might be trapped underneath."

"Is that what you expected?"

"Yes, my old boss from Princeton Fuel Oil days told me that they used a vacuum cleaner, and it was interesting to see how well it actually worked."

"What about the surface prep?"

"Looked like somebody floating concrete. I'd done that before so the whole thing was pretty interesting."

"You seemed to pay a lot of attention to the details. Was there anyone else watching the construction?"

"I was the one who was there during the daytime. Peggy Oglesby, who lived across the way, was interested. She'd come home at night from work and take a picture of the day's progress. She probably has the best visual record if she's kept them."

"I've seen you before," said the officer. The comment took McGowan by surprise. He thought for a moment about how the cop might have recognized him.

"I did the funeral for Abe Todd," he said.

It was now Bostwick's turn to go thoughtfully to another time and place. Todd was a retired cop who had been killed in an accident off Cleveland Road, and Davis had been drafted to deal with the family's tragedy.

"Of course," said the sergeant.

"Tell me," began McGowan, "why all these questions about a swimming pool repair that happened four years ago?"

"It's not about the pool," began Bostwick, "it's what was found under the pool when they pulled back the torn liner."

In a flash, images twisted and accelerated into a vortex that compressed into a compact bundle beneath a thin layer of plastic. Four years, freshly compacted soil, a troweled layer of sand, and tears running down a Goth cheek. "Brandon Carpenter," said Davis, more to himself than anyone. The sergeant had been talking, but the words stopped as McGowan spoke the name.

"The items found on the body would indicate that," said the cop, "the autopsy will make it conclusive. Did you know him?"

Chapter 15

Empty Chair

Davis had no way of contacting Ashley, and it would have been inappropriate to do so. He was her professor, not her pastor. The police may not have even contacted her family, but he doubted that. There was, however, a sensational front page headline in the *Sandusky Journal*, but the article was sparse on details, saying only that a decomposed body had been found in a swimming pool and that the police were investigating. The majority of the column was taken up, not with words, but with a picture of several patrol cars blocking the entrance to Lexington Glen. As he drove past on the access ramp to Route 2, he looked over and saw that a single vehicle was still parked by the curb and a uniformed officer was controlling traffic in and out.

Ashley's back row seat remained empty, and the two *flip-flops* noticed when they appeared in lockstep. McGowan wondered if they knew any of the news. If they did, it altered nothing in their demeanor or morning pattern. He wondered if the truth, when it came out, would be a shock to their systems. After all, the community was one press release away from finding that a conveniently absent scapegoat was also a victim. He had not escaped to the highway on his bike, and he had not sent a postcard from Vinton County. Somebody had done those things, somebody who was probably still at-large, and somebody who had been in Davis' backyard. Would a revelation about an old murder also reveal years of injustice by the tongues of a small town rumor mill?

McGowan had his own routine. After class, he walk across the quad to Founder's Hall to check his faculty mailbox. Today was not going to be an exception even though he ran into Sergeant Bostwick, who was coming out of the administrative offices. The sight of his approach gave Davis a bit of uneasiness. The county sheriff had a very visible presence on campus, but he had never seen a city cop on duty.

"Sergeant," he said with a nod, "is there any further news? Ashley Carpenter wasn't in class today."

"I wouldn't expect that she would," said Bostwick. "I came here to see if I could catch you, if you have a moment."

McGowan's mind rushed to catch up with the sudden twist that his stomach had already anticipated. *You came to catch me? Catch me at what?* was what he thought. "I can spare the time," he said, "I'm just going over to check my mail."

Bostwick reversed his course by walking with Davis back toward the building he had just vacated. "Have you seen the paper this morning?" asked the cop.

"Yes," said McGowan. "The article didn't say much."

"No, it didn't. When the victim is identified, a lot of old stuff is going to come flooding back. That's why we're being so aggressive about gathering every scrap of detail that we can. Four years ago we didn't have many leads. The killing of Aaron Fahrenhauser took place along the shore and the nearby field didn't yield much.

Later we found a bike and a canoe. Everything was pretty scattered."

Davis relaxed at the tone of the conversation. This was the closest that Bostwick had ever come toward an open explanation of what was happening and the cryptic nature of their previous encounter. This sudden ease and his cooperative nature led to an unguarded comment that he'd wished he had not spoken. Unfortunately, it was only as he heard the words coming from his own mouth that he recognized how it could be interpreted.

"And then there was that postcard."

"You know about that?" asked the officer.

"Well, Ashley told me," Davis answered realizing, too late, that this was no casual conversation. "She's my student this semester, and she told me about her brother and why she didn't think he'd sent the card."

"Do most of your students confide in you like this?"

McGowan thought about this. "No, most only worry about grades and term papers, but every once in awhile..."

"Every once in awhile, what?"

"Sometimes they're carrying something pretty heavy, and I must come across as someone who will listen. Who knows why, but they tell me a lot."

Bostwick now hesitated as if trying to decide whether it would be against procedure to step out of character. "I know Ruthie said you were very kind to the family when Abie was killed," he said referring back to the events of a year earlier when McGowan had conducted a funeral.

Davis nodded, remembering the conversations at the hospitals when the dying cop lay in a coma, and how the family had opened up to him when he was a virtual stranger. Maybe his *slip* of offering a simple truth would be understood by the investigator.

"I really came to ask about something else." Sergeant Bostwick was back in uniform. "In talking to some of the other people at the condo about the pool, somebody let slip the fact that you fronted the money for the construction. Is that true?"

Let slip? thought Davis. "It wasn't really a big deal," he said. "At the end of the winter we lost the water in the pool. We had been patching the liner for a few years trying to put off a major expense, but now it was finally beyond repair. I went to the bank to see if we could take a loan, but there would be a lot of red tape. We'd have to have an appraisal done to determine how many property assets the association had. It would take several thousand dollars to do the surveys and get through the paper work. Beth and I had some CDs in our retirement account; we just used them as collateral and took a personal loan for the repairs."

"Why would you risk that?"

"It was our home, and it wasn't that big a risk. I was the treasurer; I knew that the payment schedule was reasonable. The loans were in our name, but our money was never involved. Everything was paid back to the bank in a year, and our neighbors had a pool to enjoy rather that a stagnant mosquito-breeding bog."

"That goes along with the bank records," said Bostwick. "It's the timing that seems a bit too convenient. A kid is killed the night before a liner is placed in a pool that's located a half a mile away in a residential neighborhood. Whoever did it knew about the pool and knew how to cover their tracks so that no one suspected anything the next morning. When the workers came back to the site, they picked up where they left off the day before, and dropped the vinyl into place."

"None of that was a secret," said McGowan. "I'm sure half the people in town had heard about the pool being fixed. There was a work crew. Probably a dozen people worked on that project prior to that time."

"And they have all been accounted for," added the cop. He eyed Davis for awhile. "If you think of anything, you'll let us know, won't you?"

"Sure," said McGowan who wasn't too sure of anything at the moment.

Bostwick left him standing outside the double glass doors of Founder's Hall. Davis hid his tension by doing his normal routine. He opened the door and turned left toward the wall of mail slots with their brass front plates and combination locks.

"Dr. McGowan," came a call from the adjacent office area, "I was just about to put this note in your mailbox." The long-haired student assistant walked out to meet him. She handed him a slip of paper. It read just as he expected: *Ashley Carpenter will not be in class for awhile. The body found yesterday turned out to be her missing brother.*

Now everybody knew everything. Now everybody knew nothing.

Chapter 16

River Patrol

Sailing on weekends can be dicey, not because the lake gets crowded, but because the traffic on the Huron River becomes more congested than the roads that wind back toward the marinas tucked away upstream. Revelers are also a potential challenge. The days of going out on a boat with a cooler of beer ended years before, and yet, many revelers still try to revive the practice. The response from law enforcement in Huron was to commission a patrol boat marked after the fashion of the cruisers in order to police the waters. The end result was that those riding jet skis without life jackets could expect to be stopped, and those with booze aboard could expect a breathalyzer.

Golden Willow was docked in a berth right on the river channel which meant the helmsman had to coordinate the command to cast off the dock lines with the relative position of speedboats coming under the railway trestle and fisherman returning to the boat ramp on the eastern shore. It was early Sunday afternoon, and, by the time Darnell and Megan appeared in the marina parking lot, Beth and Davis had uncovered the sails and readied the boat for a short foray out onto the lake. The day was bright and sunny with a steady breeze from the south which meant that the water would be relatively smooth. The same might not be said for those on the Canadian side. Wave height increases with the distance the wind travels over water, and by the time the breeze hit the shores of Canada, the swells would be significantly steeper. Across the river toward the boat ramp, the gray police speedboat with two on board crept along with an eye to those backing trailers down the concrete launch ramp. Davis climbed up on the cabin top and waved his arms to attract the attention of the newly arrived guests. Darnell waved back and pointed out *Golden Willow* to Megan. They took a canvas bag from the trunk of Wilson's black Malibu and set out along the walkway toward the river.

"You found us," called McGowan.

"What kind of investigators would we be if we couldn't?" said Megan.

"Come aboard. I understand that you know your way around a boat, Megan. You might want to warn Darnell about not hesitating."

"Good idea," she answered as a confused look came over the Lakewood detective's face. "You don't want to get caught with one foot on the dock and the other one in the boat," she said taking hold of one of the stainless steel wire shrouds, placing her left foot on the boat's deck and quickly pivoting to swing her right leg aboard. The movement was so swift that Wilson could only guess at the specifics, but he had no difficulty following suit.

"I asked Megan if we had to worry about the boat rolling over, but she only laughed," said Darnell.

Beth and Davis exchanged glances. "It can roll a lot," said McGowan, "but trust me–no trust *Golden Willow*–she won't actually roll over. Will tell you about that later."

"We brought bottled water and soft drinks," said Megan, who was still toting the bag that they brought from the car.

"And we have sunscreen," said Beth.

"Already put it on," said Wilson, "Megan is trying to move me out of the *like-to-try-it-once* category and into the *want-to-know-everything* group."

"I'd be glad to help you with that, Megan," said Davis.

"Going out today, McGowan?" The voice came from the gray patrol boat with *Police* written in large black letters on the hull.

"Thought we would," answered Davis. The boat was now treading water just off the stern of *Golden Willow* and blocking any movement.

"I see you have company," said the uniformed cop with the inflatable life vest. "I assume you have the required safety equipment."

"We do," said Davis. "They just arrived and we're sorting everything out."

"Would you show me?" said the cop. McGowan did not recognize the man. It was not Bostwick, and he wondered how the officer had known him.

"Sure," he said and went down below to the hanging locker where he and Beth kept the spare life jackets and an orange tote with other emergency gear. He passed four life jackets up through the companionway where Megan took them one by one and laid them out on the cockpit benches. She did not look alarmed or scared, but Davis could see that she was trying to solve the puzzle of what was really happening.

At last McGowan stepped up out of the cabin and reached into the bag withdrawing a steel canister of compressed gas with what looked like an old bicycle horn attached. "Here's my auditory signal," he said holding it out and then setting it down on the bench near the lifejackets. He reached back into the sack to grab the handheld flares that were stowed there.

"That's okay," said the cop. "Just be careful," he said and the boat engine revved higher and they were headed back down the river and hidden behind the hulls of the longer boats docked further downstream.

"Can I ask what that was about?" said Sorento sounding more like the FBI agent she was than the bride she intended to very soon be.

"Let's get out on the water," said Davis. "After I tell you what I know, you can tell me if any of it makes sense."

The mile-and-a half journey down river took less than fifteen minutes, but the McGowans always saw new things. This was especially true when they had company aboard *Golden Willow*. Interest in the sights that had become ordinary were renewed by comments from the newbies. Among them were always the Great Blue Herons that monitored the shoreline, the Cormorants who sat on old pilings with wings spread to dry in the sun, and the thousands of gulls on the mountainous gravel piles near the lime plant.

When there was a break in the upriver lane of entering boats, Davis did a one-eighty and turned the boat back toward the direction that they had just come.

"Beth, would you take the helm?" he said as he started to walk forward to the mast. Beth took the wheel.

"I wondered if you would do that," said Sorento and only Darnell was confused. "He's going to raise the mainsail," said Megan. "The wind is from the south. If we raise the sail, we can ride the wind all the way out of the harbor."

"But why are we going back?" asked Wilson.

"We're not going back," said Sorento, "we're pointing the boat into the wind. It's the only way to hoist the sails. If we tried to do it any other way, the wind would fill the sail and there's no way that we could get it raised."

"Is the wind that strong?"

"Six tons," called Davis from the mast where he started to pull on the main halyard and the white Dacron sail began to lift with the sound of the line running through a sheave at the top of the mast.

"What does he mean by that?" asked Darnell

"You asked if the wind is powerful," said Beth. "*Golden Willow* weighs six tons and this light summer breeze is strong enough to send us to Canada if we keep the sails full and the course straight."

Darnell may have had his doubts, but they vanished when the diesel was killed. Rather than slowing down, the boat rolled slightly to one side and picked up forward momentum. Without the throb of the engine, other sounds dominated the environment. They were the sounds of wind, water, and the creaking of ropes straining in pulleys against the constant push of the wind.

"It's as I imagined," said Darnell like a kid on a field trip. "It's so smooth."

"Today it is," said Davis returning to the wheel. "Some days it's a roller coaster and the wind is so strong you'd only need a handkerchief to get you up to this speed. As the wind gets stronger, you need less sail."

"Wouldn't you just go really fast?"

"Doesn't work that way," said McGowan. "The sails are the engines that push us through the water, but the water is pushing back. Eventually, the water says *that's fast enough*. It's kinda like sticking your hand out the car window when you're driving. You can hold your palm out against the air pressure when you're going twenty, but at eighty, you'd better put it sideways or it'll turn you around."

"You should have both hands on the wheel," said Wilson.

"Yes, officer," said Davis, "and a sailor needs less sail area. When we get safely back to shore, Beth and I will tell you why that's a good lesson to learn."

"Speaking of learning," interrupted Megan, "what was happening at the dock? That guy wasn't interested in any safety inspection."

"No," agreed Wilson, "he had you in his sights from the time he came up behind us. Is he a friend of yours?"

"Never met him," said McGowan, "but he knew who I was. I think he was telling me that I am being watched."

"Is it about the body that was found last week?" asked Megan. "It was the brother of your student, wasn't it?"

"Yes, it was."

"How's the family holding up?"

"I don't know. It's all come down very suddenly. Ashley wasn't in class. I sent her an email, but otherwise, I have no direct way to contact her. No funeral plans have been mentioned."

"I'd guess that the body hasn't been released by the coroner," said Wilson.

"But what has that to do with you? You're Ashley's professor. The harbor patrol has something else in mind."

Davis and Beth exchanged glances. "What's the cliché? No good deed goes unpunished? I've been tied to the swimming pool where the body was discovered. Beth and I had a condo there. I was on the board, signed the contract for the job, and monitored the project. They seem to think I might know more than I do."

"Maybe you do," said Wilson.

The comment surprised Davis. "What do…"

"Most witnesses know more than they can easily remember," Megan added. "You were there around the time it happened. You might have seen more than you thought."

"I've wracked my brain thinking back over those days," said McGowan. "One day the bottom was shaped with a trowel, the next day they dropped in a liner. That's it."

"How about a year later?" asked Darnell, "anything happen then?"

"A year later?"

"If I buried a body somewhere, I might check it now and again," said Megan who had originally met Darnell on a similar case when they first worked together. He was a Lakewood detective, and she an unofficial profiler on loan from the Cleveland Division of the FBI.

"Is that how it works?" asked Davis.

"A lot of serial killers use the same dumping grounds. If it worked before… well, they stay with what works. I doubt if this guy is a serial killer, *under* a swimming pool is a little too hard to arrange. It had to be someone who knew the area and who knew the timing on the project. Maybe a construction worker?"

"Apparently, they've all been cleared," said Davis. "Don't ask me how."

"That leaves all the rest of your neighbors. How many condos are there?"

"Thirty-six," said Davis. "It's a small development. Half are octogenarians, a lot of them have long commutes to work or own it like we did at first–it's a second home for weekends or summer."

"And so you are left standing," said Sorento.

"And the cheese stands alone!" said McGowan.

"Well, at least that's in your favor."

Davis turned at Wilson's comment. His confused expression begged the question: *What's in my favor?*

"I only mean," continued Darnell, "that whoever did this wasn't standing alone. The kid who was killed was a football player. I'm sure he wasn't pro-sized, but–and I don't mean any offense– too heavy for you to handle by yourself. How'd you do it? Dig a hole, carry a hundred-and-eighty pounds over the side, fill the hole, and smooth it over so that no one would guess the next morning. Did Beth help?" Though it was gallows humor, the image made its point.

"Thank you for that," said Davis. "Of course you're right, though, I've known of circumstantial cases that blew out of control. At least being a ninety-pound weakling is in my favor."

"You've got to remember," said Wilson, "that the police are in a pressure cooker right now. They had an open case for four years, but the case was cold and everybody knew, or thought they knew, exactly what happened. Now all of a sudden, their presumed on-the-run murderer is a second victim and the killer or killers have been on the loose for four years. They need a theory."

"And here I am," said Davis.

"They may be right about one thing, though. You may have seen more than you know. Stop playing the record of that time period in your head. Ever see anyone just hanging around who shouldn't have been there?"

Megan had not been adding much to Darnell's investigative suggestions. When she finally spoke, her voice was soft under the rush of the wind off the sails.

"If Ashley needs someone to talk to, I know what she's going through." The comment turned McGowan's thoughts around completely.

"I'll mention it to her," he said. "Thanks."

Chapter 17

Beach Glass

While sailing, Davis had been able to speak with the couple about the wedding that was scheduled for June. In fact, McGowan intentionally set a western course when they had cleared the Huron light, and conversation turned abruptly from a river patrol to the wedding when he pointed out a stretch of coastline that held a gazebo and an obvious open view of the lake.

"That's Sawmill Creek," he said, pointing toward a low breakwall and a few masts jutting above the great boulders.

"Could we go in there on this boat?" asked Wilson.

"It's more for powerboats and shallow draft sailboats. I'm afraid we'd run aground."

From this watery vantage point, however, they could envision the ceremony and were glad that they had made the decision to locate their wedding in the small town. As if to seal the deal, a bald eagle made an appearance, flying low, and parallel to the land's edge.

As they later said their good-byes, Davis asked one final question of the couple.

"Should I get a lawyer?" The two looked at each other as if exchanging telepathic messages.

"I can't advise you," began Darnell with a cautious hesitation in his voice. "They may not suspect you at all, but they're pushing everybody to come up with something new that they can follow." The words were somewhat reassuring, but a caveat was tagged to them. "On the other hand, they'll expect a guilty person to panic. They're only human. You push back too hard and they may jump."

"Better not to tell them much about your sailing passengers," added Megan.

"Why's that?"

"If they think you're reaching out to other jurisdictions—well, that's a power play. Getting a lawyer is a civilian's defensive posture. Bringing in your own army is a direct assault, and we couldn't help you there. Our departments would come down on us, not them."

"I can see that," said McGowan, "you're just a nervous bride."

"No," said Darnell, "that's Agent Sorento. I'm the nervous one!"

The laughter that followed led to a flurry of best wishes and promises to meet again soon. Beth and Davis found themselves staring at the retreating image of a black car slowly navigating a speed bump across the marina drive that ran out to the main street.

"How 'bout taking the long way home?" said Beth. Davis agreed. While the sail had been perfect from a technical point of view, other events continued to trouble the couple.

They set out on a familiar route that took them through a gap in the marina's perimeter fence, across the yacht club, boat basin, and along the river walkway. They set the river to their backs and cut across a field toward the bowling alley and then to Lakefront Park. Here, there was a public beach, but there were no swimmers. While the sun was warm, the water was cold and the only one brave enough to challenge the chill was a border collie who was intent on bringing a favorite stick back to his master only to have it thrown again into the deep. A second dog stood ashore as if assessing the sanity of the other breed.

"This doesn't offer much hope for finding anything," said Davis. Beth understood the cryptic remark. This beach was one of the many places to look for beach glass, the somewhat gemological name for broken bottles that were lake-polished and washed ashore. Collected by all the area beachcombers, larger pieces found their way into various craft projects and jewelry sold in shops and at street fairs. This time of day, however, the selection would be limited to tiny camouflaged brown glass, bits nearly indistinguishable from the round stones that had ground them smooth.

"Let's try the other beach," suggested Beth.

Huron, like any coastal community, had been shaped by the vagaries of the water. The jagged north edge of the park belied the early city planners who laid out the plot as a public square. To the north ran the less than creatively named, North Street. Beyond that was a neighborhood known as Piety Hill where the who's who of Huron settled, but not for long. Erie had other ideas and erosion claimed North Street and the foundations of the homes that were not moved inland. That was more than a century before the McGowans came to town, and explained why the most northerly road that ran more than two blocks was called South Street.

The changing coastline also created a second beach that was west of the old town center and tucked back behind a residential neighborhood. Since there was no immediate public parking nearby, the place was mainly known to locals and became a destination for high schoolers looking for a private spot to party on summer evenings. The McGowans didn't know if there was an actual name for the place, but they had heard it referred to as West Cove. Here the beach was a long expanse facing north into the open lake. Getting to it, however, was always an issue in the early spring.

They walked along South until it ended where the way was blocked by a small stream and then they turned right on West Street that paralleled the little creek north to the lake and to where a small cut-through the undergrowth gave them the first glimpse of the hidden shore. This was where they would find out if they would even make it to the sandy strand.

In mid-summer, the streambed would be dry with hardly a trickle of the inland run-off making it to the lake. With spring rains, however, the waters usually flowed with such force that it would float away any temporary logs or boards nailed in place to serve neighbors looking to walk along the private beach. With the recent rain, the McGowans fully expected knee deep rushing currents to discourage their quest for beach glass, but this time they were in luck. The bridge that they found in place spanned a greater distance than the stream required and looked as though it had been engineered to be more permanent than the makeshift structures of the past.

"They must be trying to open the beach for more public use," observed Davis. They crossed over the span and walked across the broad beach to where the water lapped against the shore.

"Obviously, the geese like it here," said Davis as he stepped carefully to avoid a minefield of droppings.

The view of the lake was so unobstructed compared to Lakefront Park. Still, the spoil area that created the small bay which sheltered the more public beach could be seen off to the right. Beth was wandering along the surf as Davis' mind wandered somewhere else.

"That's where that kid Aaron was murdered," he said pointing to the spoil area.

"Do you think that's where Ashley's brother was also killed?" asked Beth.

"I doubt it," said Davis, "whoever did it would have had to carry his body back down the pier and across town to get it over to Lexington Glen. That's a long, public haul."

"Wasn't there a canoe?" Beth's comment triggered a chain reaction.

"You're right," said Davis. "It's so simple. They didn't have to carry anything very far. They just used the canoe."

"They?"

"Darnell said it," replied McGowan. "One person couldn't dig a hole and get the body down into the pool. So they'd have more than one person to help with a canoe. That little stream that we just walked over, it gets narrow just before it dumps into the lake and that makes the water run fast. But it's quieter just a little upstream, isn't it?"

Beth had to think for a moment. All these little run-offs meandered through neighborhoods, ducked under roads through drain pipes, and reappeared blocks away. Where did this one flow?

"This one must go under the bridge on Cleveland Road," she offered. "And you're right. There, at the bridge, it looks more like a pond than a stream."

"What about south of the bridge?" asked Davis. Again, Beth thought. They had walked the sidewalks on both sides of that span. On the north were cattails and water plants that sheltered ducks, but to the south the terrain was quite different. It was a grassy low area where the stream bed was narrow and ran straight back into a wooded area beyond which were homes and neighborhoods.

"This is Washburn Ditch," she said in recognition. "If they could get across Cleveland Road, the creek runs right alongside of Lexington Glen."

"Or under the bridge," said Davis.

"Or under it," agreed Beth. "If the pipes under the bridge are big enough, they could have paddled a canoe straight through."

"I'll bet they are," said Davis, "but there's so much overgrowth along the water, I don't know where anyone could see that."

"Which means that they'd be pretty invisible at night, but the water could be moving fast and it would be dark–could it be done?"

Davis smiled. "Well, a year ago, I would have had my doubts, but I've been to Kenya."

"An African could find a way to get it done," she agreed. They hurried back over the bridge and retraced their steps to South Street. They risked a bit of trespassing by sneaking into the last yard on the block and made their way to a small cutout that afforded a glimpse of where the roadway crossed the water. The culverts under the road were six or eight feet wide, certainly wide enough for a canoe. Just beyond the field on the upstream side were the trees that skirted the condos where they had lived for several years.

"It *is* Washburn Ditch," said Beth quietly.

"No," said Davis, "I think it's a secret escape; it's McGowan's Pass."

Chapter 18

Over the Phone

Thanks to Beth, Davis had a theory as to how a body could be moved invisibly across town to a secret burial site. Though it was also purely conjecture on his part, going directly to the police would only heighten their already elevated curiosity about his involvement. The better part of valor at this point was to stick with trying to remember any suspicious behavior that he might have observed around the time of the killing and the years that followed. His internal debate was whether he should chance going back to Lexington Glen in an effort to mentally retrace his life there. On the one hand, he might remember something that would be helpful in the case. On the other, if he was being watched, it might be attributed to his need to return to the scene of *his* crime. The back and forth argument waged inside his mind ended suddenly with a ring of his phone.

"Dr. McGowan," came a small voice, "this is Ashley Carpenter."

"Yes, Ashley," he said, "I heard the news about your brother. I'm so sorry." The pause at the other end grew uncomfortable. "Are you still there?"

"Yes," she said. "I knew that he had to be dead, but there was still a part of me that hoped he was alive. Now, to find this out..."

"I don't understand it myself," said Davis. "Is there anything I can do to help?"

"The police have been here. They talked to all of us. Asked a lot of questions."

"They're working hard to try and figure out what might have happened."

"I suppose so, but what surprised me is that they asked if we knew you. My Mom and Dad said they didn't, and I didn't realize that they were talking about you, at first. They said that you knew me, but I was confused. They said you were a *reverend* who lived in Huron. Finally, one of them called you *doctor* and I realized who they were talking about. They said that you could tell me about the place where Brandon was found."

Davis hesitated before answering. *Was some sort of game being played here with Ashley in the middle?*

"Yes, I used to live in those condos at the time when the pool liner was installed," said McGowan. "I can't say that I know much more than that." (He wasn't about to reveal his and Beth's more recent conjecture.)

"Can you show me the place?" she asked in a shaky voice.

"Of course, if that's what you want."

"I think I do. And I think my Dad will want to after he thinks about it for awhile."

"Ashley," said Davis. "I have a friend who lives over in Cleveland. I trust her a lot and I told her a little bit about what happened to your brother. It turns out that her brother was killed when she was in high school, and somebody reached out to her then and it made all the difference. Anyway, she said if you ever wanted to talk..."

"Is she another reverend or a shrink?" asked Carpenter.

Now it was Davis' turn to hesitate. "Actually, she's with the FBI." McGowan stopped there, letting it sink in.

"Is she trying to find out who did this to my brother?"

"Not directly," said Davis. "She's getting married in June. Her fiancé is a cop in Lakewood. They're just really fine people. I'm going to be the minister at their wedding–that's why I've been with them lately–she just thought that you two might have a lot in common. Anyway, if you'd be willing… well, I think she might help you a lot."

They agreed to meet the next morning, and Ashley seemed anxious to meet with Megan, though perhaps for the wrong reason. Having the FBI on the case seemed more hopeful than the local police, but Davis knew that was a fiction. The lines between jurisdictions were carefully drawn, and it would be Megan, not Agent Sorento, who would be talking to the Goth girl.

A call to Megan's cell phone also brought quick results. Tomorrow she was on desk patrol, and felt sure that her supervisor would let her break away from the paperwork for a few hours in the morning.

Nothing about this made Davis relax. While Ashley's family had to be the first consideration, he felt a continuing uneasiness about being drawn back into a murder investigation.

The evening air was chilly, but the chicken parmesan that they cooked in the oven warmed the house nicely. As they sat to eat their late supper, the phone then interrupted one more time. This time it was Matt Fornesby calling to say that his father and stepmother were in Cleveland and could the four of them drive over for a visit on Tuesday. All the local weather forecasts were still offering prognostications of clear skies and warm readings. "Sure," said Davis, "we'll be looking forward to it."

He put the phone back in the charger. "The Fornesbys will be coming over on Tuesday afternoon," he said to his wife.

"It'll be good to see them again," she said. "I really did enjoy meeting Molly."

McGowan's thoughts went back to the death of Barker's first wife, Angie. Perhaps his meeting with his old friend would be the parallel to Megan and Ashley's. If anyone could understand his present inner turmoil, it would be Barker Fornesby. He said nothing to Beth, however. There were things that she would never know.

Chapter 19

Lexington Glen

When Davis turned off the city street and onto the private road that was the entrance to Lexington Glen, he saw the pool straight ahead and on the right. The perimeter was still cordoned off with yellow plastic crime scene tape, and he recognized the woman standing just outside the barrier line. It was Megan Sorento. She had agreed to be here and assist Ashley Carpenter in coming to grips with the insanity that was violent crime. He turned left and pulled into a space usually reserved for visitors.

"Did you just get here, or have you had a chance to look around?" he asked as he approached Sorento.

She gave him a glance and turned back to the hole that had been a swimming pool.

"It's a secondary crime scene," she observed. "I doubt if anything happened here other than the body being dumped. Where were you living at the time?"

She sounded like an investigating officer rather than a bride-to-be, but McGowan understood the connection. "Over there," he said pointing to the building to the immediate left of the pool. Though it was closest to the pool, it was oriented the opposite direction so that the doors and windows did not open with a clear view of the area.

She stood silently for a few more moments before speaking. "Which direction would they come from?" she asked. "The normal routes are fairly public and open. If they came in from the drive, they'd be in plain sight. Was this fence around the pool area during reconstruction?" She was looking at the chain link mesh that encompassed the swim area.

"They had it down during that time," said McGowan. "They had to get heavy equipment in there to tear out the old concrete."

"I figured that," she said. "That means that they didn't have to go in by the gate. They could come from the back and avoid the street where people might be watching for cars entering. What's back there? Looks like houses mostly."

"It's all residential," Davis began, "it's heavily planted to give a visual barrier. There's also another chain link fence–basically runs the entire perimeter."

"Basically?"

She had picked up his unconscious equivocation. *Why did the word come out so easily?* It was a perimeter fence, but there were breaks in it, three to be exact.

"I guess because it doesn't go all the way around," he said thinking about the places where the barrier wasn't deemed necessary. The front of the property was bounded by a grassy drainage ditch the ran down to the creek which was a second unfenced area. To the south was a dense thicket beyond which was the high school. There was at least one path through the trees that was sometimes used by students cutting through. They would then jump the fence on the back property line or walk its full length to cross over Washburn Ditch when the water was low.

"I guess it doesn't really surround it," said Davis, "it just runs along the north property line. Beth and I have an idea how the body was brought here, and actually, it avoids the roads altogether." Megan turned to face him as if trying to take a clue from his facial expression. The scrutiny called for elaboration.

"We were down on the beach at West Cove. There's a place where a run-off dumps into the lake. That's when we realized that it's the little creek that runs along the east side of the property. From what Beth found in the newspapers, there was a canoe involved–it was used by the kid who was first killed and turned up a week or so later. Anyway, we figured that the body could have been placed in the canoe and then paddled or pulled upstream. Once they hit our property line, it's just a gently sloping lawn up here to poolside."

"And so they could come around from behind, and avoid the more public driveway and parking areas."

"They could," agreed Davis. "There's a security light between those two buildings," he added, pointing to a free standing metal antenna tower between two condos. "So I think they'd follow along the edge of the back fence."

"Where the plantings would shield them from view of the houses in the adjoining neighborhood," said Megan.

"That's my current guess," said Davis who looked up in time to see a gray and black police cruiser turn into the lane. "Looks like we have company."

"I suggest you not tell him your theory just yet," said Sorento. "We need to think it through better. Otherwise, they may jump to the conclusion that you are trying to distract them from your suspicious behavior."

"Right," said Davis sarcastically. "How should I introduce you?"

"Don't," she said. "I'm not here in any official way. He doesn't need to know anything unless he asks specifically."

"Returning to the scene," said Sergeant Bostwick as he stepped nearer the pair. McGowan could not detect either irony or humor in his inflection so he did not know how to respond.

"Actually, Ashley Carpenter asked me to meet her here," said Davis. "She had heard that I used to live here and wanted me to be with her when she came to see where they found her brother."

"You'd be the best one to show her," said the cop. This time Davis caught a more cynical tone and knew that he shouldn't be feeling any love.

"I used to live here," he said. "And, thanks to somebody from your department, she knows that I was also around when the new liner was placed here. Is that what you mean?"

"You tell me," said the officer, then as if changing the subject: "Did you know that cadaver dogs can detect where bodies were placed years ago, even after they've been moved." Megan's eyes darted quickly to the officer and then to McGowan. She had either guessed or wanted to hear what would come next.

"It's pretty clear where the body was found," said Davis. "You wouldn't need a bloodhound for that."

"We were trying to figure out where the body had been *before* it ended up in that hole. The guy who bought your condo was very cooperative, didn't even have to ask for a warrant. He just opened the door and let us bring in the dog."

"So?"

"You tell me."

"Tell you what?" asked Davis.

"Tell me why he sniffed a bit and then sat down. That's how these dogs indicate a hit. The dog told us that a body had been laid on that carpet at one time. If I'm correct, it's the carpet that you had installed when you first bought the place."

"Maybe the new guy clipped his toenails there," interjected Megan.

Bostwick turned to her as if seeing her for the first time. "That's a plot from a silly detective novel," he said. "Cadaver dogs don't make mistakes, honey."

Davis almost felt sorry for the hapless cop. "First, they are called HRD's, not cadaver dogs. That's Human Remains Detection dogs. I've seen a few really good ones in my time, but they are rare," she continued. "The dogs are only as good as their handlers, and sometimes respond to other biosensors if the pre-search investigators get sloppy."

"Your chippy friend has a mouth on her," he said turning to McGowan.

"I think she knows her stuff," replied Davis, "and it's your mouth that's going to get into trouble."

"Who are you?" the cop said, turning to Sorento.

"I said *unless he asks*, didn't I?" Davis nodded to Megan when she turned to him. She turned back to face the officer, a hand going to the back pocket of her slacks and pulling out a credentials wallet.

"I am not here in any official capacity," she began. "You asked me for some identification, and I am complying with your request. I was here talking with my friend, and you made a backhanded accusation without advising him of his rights. You called me a *chippy* which, if I'm not mistaken, means that I'm either a little street whore or cute as a chipmunk. Since I have been told that I am cute, I'll ignore the tough-cop bullying–I'm sure your captain would prefer that to a complaint." She flipped open the wallet. "I am Agent Sorento, Cleveland Division of the FBI. We are issued the smallest badges in law enforcement, but you'll find this one's very real. Now, would you like me to tell you about HRD's? I have been personally introduced to two of the best, Maggie and Dixie. Oh, maybe I should have put it down on your level–let's just pretend and call them *cadaver dogs.*"

McGowan was never one to take delight in someone else's suffering, but he felt a twinge of joy at this particular moment. He also was overwhelmed by the sense that one of the three of them had an immense urge to run, and it was the one wearing the badge and uniform.

"Look," said Sorento. "You didn't deserve that–you asked for it, but you didn't deserve it. Like I said, I'm not here in any capacity other than that I offered to talk to one of Dr. McGowan's students. I once lost a brother in a similar way, and someone helped me back then. I'm just returning the favor.

"Davis is a smart man. Actually, he helped me and my partner break a murder investigation once. If I understand even a little of what's happened, he may be your best witness. He doesn't need to be pushed; he needs time to think with a clear head. Isn't that right, Davis?"

McGowan nodded, and the three stood like triangulated pillars of stone until Bostwick extended his hand to McGowan.

"We've never had an answer to this crime," he began, "but everybody in town had the story figured out in such a way that they could fix the blame on a bad guy who was no longer around. Everybody slept well at night, and nobody blamed us for not laying hands on the perp."

"Then the perp became the second victim. Murder-suicide would have been an acceptable answer, but he couldn't have buried himself and graded the pool behind him," said Davis.

"Which means," said the cop, "that there's a killer or killers at large, and we're the stupid ones who didn't see it in the first place."

"And I was here," said McGowan, "and this semester I had a troubled girl who always wears black sitting in the back row. You'd like to answer for the city; I'd like to give Ashley some answers."

"And the FBI was *never* here," said Megan. "Do we have a truce, then?"

"What I really want is evidence," said Bostwick. "I might only have a pile of toenail clippings at this point."

The three laughed at no one's expense. A lone figure was walking down the drive. She was wearing all black.

"Ashley's here," announced Davis. Sergeant Bostwick took his leave and went back to where the patrol car was parked.

"Wonder how he'll report *this*?" said Megan.

"If he reports it at all," said McGowan.

"He will," she said. "I can tell he's a good cop. He just guessed wrong on a strategy that would rattle your cage."

"Funny, I thought he was doing a good job at that! You brought him down pretty well."

"I'd appreciate your not telling anybody about that," she confided. "Didn't exactly conform to agency policies on interacting with local jurisdictions. On the other hand, he did say *chippy*."

"Yes, he did," said McGowan, "and he paid the price."

"Yes, he did," said Sorento. "But we're supposed to manage and measure our response. That one felt too good."

Ashley was anxious to see the place where her brother's body had been found. She accepted a hug from Megan, but the tears that could not be held back spoke of first things first. Davis led the way.

While they could not pass the taped perimeter, they could view the roughly excavated depression exposed where the liner was cut away. They joined hands and stood in silence for a long period before Ashley turned back. Her first question was directed to Megan.

"Dr. McGowan says that you're an FBI agent. Can you tell me what is going on?"

"Do you mean about the investigation?"

"I guess. I mean, I don't know. Why haven't they let us have my brother's body?"

"I don't know any specifics about this," Sorento began, "but I do know that they will test everything they can that will give them clues as to what happened. I know that doesn't do anything to help what you're feeling."

"I don't know what I'm feeling."

"I remember being angry and sad when they found my brother," said Megan. "Even though he was dead, I wanted him home."

It was clear to Davis that these two would soon be talking openly and honestly about losses that, though separated by years, would join them now. He wandered away for a moment allowing the two women to talk. Though he never left their sight, he moved to the grassy lawn that sloped down toward Washburn Ditch. Even now, the water was running, not as a heavily rushing stream in a spring flood, but as a steady flow. It was definitely deep enough to float a canoe, and, if not wide enough to paddle, it could certainly be pulled along on a rope painter.

It would be easier with a couple of lines attached, thought Davis, *but that would mean having an entire crew of murderers or accomplices. Maybe that was the single detail which clouded this investigation. The imagined possibilities were limited to what a single person could do, but maybe they should have been looking for a team.* He already knew that there was a team who, in their adolescent way, hated or were jealous of Brandon Carpenter, but *could that lead to homicide? And, could such a fraternity of guilt maintain a four year silence? Wouldn't someone have cracked or confided in someone else?*

He thought about the *flip-flops* and their merciless attitude toward Ashley. He thought about his own years in small towns and trying to referee church squabbles. The old riddle popped into his head: Why are church fights so vicious? *Because there is so little at stake.*

The value of any victory is colored by the smallness of the group. To be the star quarterback at Winsted is a sort of pinnacle, but only for one year and in a very small space. It's all relative.

His reverie was broken by the sound of a gasoline engine. Though the early spring had fended off the snow plows, it awakened the lawn mowers from their winter hibernation. The landscapers were coming over the ridge with their small tractors. McGowan had already mown his grass twice; the acreage here at Lexington Glen was probably getting its second or third shearing.

Darnell had put the question to him asking if he had ever seen anyone hanging around who shouldn't have been there. Evidently, killers periodically check the security of the dumpsite. At the time, Davis could not remember anything, but now an image came to mind. He remembered once walking out toward the road with Beth. There was a young man with a pickup truck who seemed to be looking around. The truck had a bed full of small power mowers, and McGowan asked if the stranger was looking for anyone particular.

"No," said the man, and here Davis struggled to remember the exact words. He had asked something about the boundaries of the property and whether the condo association used landscapers to mow. McGowan was the treasurer at that time and knew all the answers. The man then asked if his company could make a bid. That was no problem as far as Davis was concerned, but they already had a contract for the current year and wouldn't change midseason.

"Next year, then?" The man had suggested, and he wrote down the PO Box number and promised to mail in a bid before winter. No bid had ever come, and McGowan had dismissed it simply for the fact that the mowers in the back of the truck might have been suited for typical residential properties, but they were not industrial grade. They were hardly adequate for grounds the size of Lexington Glen. The encounter did not seem suspicious. The stranger seemed to have a reasonable purpose for being there, but was the purpose what it seemed? Davis now wondered.

He looked back to where Ashley and Megan had been talking. The conversation seemed to be over, and the two were walking together toward where he stood. Sorento's arm was around the younger girl's shoulder.

"Ashley has something she needs to ask," said Megan.

Carpenter looked back toward the pool as she spoke. "We'd like to have a service or something," she said at last. "We want to bring him home and bury him with some kind of honor. Could you do that?"

Davis stepped toward her and gave her a hug as an answer. "I'll do whatever I can."

Megan filled in some of the information gaps. "They have been told that the body will be released in a day or two. They know that there can be no viewing, but they'd like to do something–I'm not sure they know all the options."

"How about I call your folks and we set up a time to talk?" said McGowan.

"That would be good. As it is, we've all just been sitting around the house waiting."

"I'll call right now," said Davis. "How about this afternoon?" There was really no need to make a call. Ashley knew the family would welcome Davis, and she provided the directions to her home.

I guess I'll finally see Winsted, thought Davis. "We saw you walk in. Do you need a ride somewhere?" he asked.

"No," said Carpenter, "I parked around the block. It's a trick I use. Walking alone gives me time to think. I need some of that right now."

With that goodbyes were all spoken, and Megan and Davis watched her head away toward the street.

"She's a tough kid," said Sorento. "Maybe I see myself in her."

"I can see the resemblance," agreed McGowan. "While you two were talking I had a few ideas about what might have happened. I have to check out a couple of things first."

"Nothing you want to share with the FBI, though."

"Not yet," said Davis. "And maybe not with the FBI so much as off the record with Agent Sorento," he added as if correcting himself.

"Do you want to hear the really sick thing?" she added. "Darnell and I feel more comfortable with an investigation than walking down an aisle in front of guests and saying, *I do*!"

"We'll work on that, too," said Davis.

Chapter 20

Winsted

Preparing for a funeral was like taking a trip back in time. Davis always found it a little distressing when, following a service, people would say that it really came through that he knew the deceased very well. The truth was that he had buried many strangers. As in this case, circumstances would draw him into a circle of grief, grief that he could appreciate and understand, but not fully share.

According to the now sympathetic news reports, the discovery of Brandon's body meant closure for a family that had been living suspended between hope and fear. The hope that he was alive only served to confirm the opinion of those who called him *fugitive* and *murderer*. They feared, however, that he was already dead, and had privately mourned his death while another family grieved over Aaron Fahrenhauser, a boy they had not known. From everything that Ashley shared, he was Brandon's friend. When the press had confirmed, in writing, the popular gossip, the Carpenters were exiled from Fahrenhauser's funeral. They didn't believe their son capable of what was being said. Yet, if the ugliness were true, he was alive somewhere. If their hearts were right, then Aaron's death was doubly painful.

"Closure" is such a misleading word, thought Davis. It was only *closure* for those who didn't know or love. It's a feel-good term for those who want to deny the reality of loss. If the book is closed, it's done. If the story is over, *get over it* is the next injustice poured on the victims. Fact was that this proof of innocence meant a violent death confirmed.

McGowan never met Brandon, and he would now have to rely on his old pastoral trick. He would have to *listen*. It was a skill more difficult to master than mouthing platitudes. It meant entering the emotional space of the family in order to hear the thoughts and feelings that ran beneath the words.

The Carpenters were no exception in that they wanted to banish the images that imagination now presented. They did not want to see a death. They retreated, instead, to a flurry of anecdotes—a little boy who was impatient, who wanted a two-wheeler before he had outgrown a big-wheeled trike. He liked running and throwing and protecting his little sister.

The price of pastoral care is pain borrowed from other people. The textbooks talked about keeping emotional distance. The textbooks were crap.

A therapist might be able to keep the indifference, becoming inured through the writing of verbatim transcripts that could be studied like something out of a doctoral dissertation. They also kept rigid boundaries. Their clients were not their friends. They did not socialize, and, if the idea ever crept in that, under *other* circumstances this person *could* have been a friend, that was a fiction that ended when the therapeutic hour ended.

Ministers lived in a different reality. They were to both weep and rejoice with a community that knew their address and phone number and did not hesitate to call. Faking it was always an option, but one that in time left the fraud empty to speak anything that resembled truth.

Truth was easy in this family. He had heard it before from Ashley who had, for some reason, trusted his ears to hear her. Her parents were no different. The gift he brought was someone who had never participated in the demonizing of their son. They could tell their story and their hopes without fighting a battle to be deemed worthy of grief. This was not closure. It was the beginning, and they brought him yearbooks and boxes of photos that had been squirreled away in closets. He let them give voice to everything, and he sat quietly when the tears trumped all other vocal expression.

"We're sorry," they said when their energy subsided.

Sorry for what? he thought. *I'm sorry that anyone would have to accept this. I don't know if I could bear it myself.* But what he said instead was: "You love him very much." He spoke his words in the present tense. It was clear that giving up love was never going to define the crock called *closure*.

They then spoke about the service that had been scheduled. They assumed it would be small and fairly private. Neighbors, even the ones who had erected a polite wall around them, were not likely to come.

"Could I borrow this?" asked McGowan who was holding up Brandon's junior yearbook. "I'll bring it back."

"Of course," said Brandon's mother. Perhaps she assumed that the handwritten comments from his few friends would help Davis get to know the son they knew. Then again, by taking the book, he was assuring that he would talk with them again.

As McGowan walked back to his car, he took stock of the neighborhood. Many of the homes in this part of the county were old farmhouses set on large lots. Here, it was clear, that someone in the sixties had partitioned a field and built a double row of split-levels. By more contemporary standards, these were still older homes, but they sat here as an oasis of modernity in the midst of cornfields. In all likelihood, one of them belonged to a family they had met on Kelley's Island.

Chapter 21

Marconi's

For all the years that Beth and Davis had known Barker Fornesby, this was the first time that he had ever been to their house. It was an isolation that was born of circumstance rather than decision. Barker moved in circles of the rich and powerful as indicated by the dinner in the surprise restaurant at JFK. The McGowans, on the other hand, were more apt to be carrying a covered dish into a church supper than socializing in one of the private dining rooms at Kitty's next to the Victoria Theater in Dayton where they had first met.

In some ways, their choice of professions sealed their schedules. Fornesby's time was considered so precious that corporations sometimes sent private jets to shuttle him to board meetings. McGowan's time was divided. While church boards reflected the *right-now* attitude of a culture unaccustomed to waiting, for the bedridden and hospitalized time slowed down as the nearness of death approached light speed. Davis always considered this a proof of Einstein's theory that time slowed as acceleration approached the limits of physics. There were times when he would sit with a parishioner knowing that a pile of phone messages were mounting on his desk and in the voice mail files of his disabled cell phone. Often, there was nothing that could be done for the patient, and he provided nothing more than the security of a companion who was confident that transitions between life and death matter more than fast answers to questions that would be meaningless in a week.

Barker was one of the powerbrokers who understood the various pacing that was life. There had been a time when he was the one that Davis accompanied during a night of waiting, and he defended his pastor against those who likened his position to the CEO of a small corporation. "Yes," he would argue, "our pastor is our chief administrator, but he is also the key player in the program staff. We want him to be able to read our balance sheet, but where we really need him is to be the spiritual guide to what we believe."

Barker won most of the arguments, not because he could illustrate it on a table of organization, but because everyone knew of his experience when his first wife, Angie, died at home.

Molly continued to impress Beth, and she could see how the couple was reinventing their personal life, moving into retirement with investment resources that were being converted to educational travel and personal philanthropy. She and Davis had done the same, but the scale was quite diminished. They lived in a small house in a quiet town, or at least a town that had been quiet until a set of bones announced their appearance.

Still, she was very pleased when Molly said, "I envy what you have here. It's the sort of life Barker and I enjoy, too."

"Matt says this town is in a bit of an uproar," noted Barker, "a body found under a swimming pool?"

"My swimming pool," said McGowan.

"Yours?"

"Well, the condo association where we lived when we moved here. I was on the board when the liner was placed in the pool, and the police think I was the site supervisor."

"Were you?"

"They were quite interested in me for awhile at least. I think they were keeping a pretty close tab on my movements."

"Did you know the kid who was killed?"

"Not at the time. His sister is a student of mine over at Firelands College. I met with her family the other day. They've asked me to conduct a memorial service."

"So now you know the family. You were at the crime scene at the time of death, and the police have been following you. Who's going to bail out your behind when they come for you?"

Davis recognized the veiled reference. He had been the bailer when Matt was in high school and Barker was trying to pull his life back together after the death of Angie.

"They have opportunity, but not motive," said McGowan sounding like a TV defense attorney.

"As you well know, Dr. McGowan, motives can be invented by people who want crimes bundled into nicely wrapped packages."

Barker's comment created a backwash of silence until, at last, Davis spoke.

"I was not at the crime scene. No one has suggested that the murder took place here. It's the place where the body was dumped after the killing."

"So, at worst, you accepted delivery on the package."

"Actually," countered Davis whose growing discomfort made him realize that he was more involved with this than he would have wished in a saner moment. *Was the memorial service going to reinsert him into the thinking of*

Bostwick? "You were the one who told me how the body arrived at the construction site."

"Me?"

"Remember you told me about my hypothetical ancestor's tavern in Central Park?"

"In the place called McGown's Pass? Sure, I remember."

"Beth and I found the pass here, or at least, its equivalent, a sort of backdoor in and out of the property. It's a small stream that runs down to the lake by the condo. There was another murder around that time–out on a little peninsula called the *spoil area*. For years, the kid whose body was found under my pool was blamed for the other killing."

"Obviously, there were two murders," said Barker who was jumping ahead on the analysis. "Potentially one was used to cover the other. Did you know the other victim?"

"Still trying to find a motive that will fit me?" said McGowan.

"I'm just being a devil's advocate or a district prosecutor, you decide which."

"No, I didn't know the other person–it was another kid. Anyway, I figure they brought the body up from the lake in a canoe that they could paddle, pull, and finally portage up to poolside."

"They? Are you dealing with a gang?"

"Actually," began Davis, "I think I'm dealing with a team." The look on Fornesby's face told Davis that the sudden turn in his story had brought about some whiplash. "It's all speculation on my part," he continued, "and it's all about adolescent jealousy, but that sort of thing happens."

"And no one has put this together until you came along?"

"There was no reason to, that is, until the second body appeared." Davis knew that these last words were undeniable. As long as it was thought that Brandon Carpenter was on the run or had committed suicide in some remote place, the case was straightforward and not mysterious.

"Do you have a particular team in mind?"

"Actually, I do–a high school football team from the next county. There was a quarterback rivalry…"

"So as part of their training regimen they carried a dead weight through McGowan's Pass. They buried it, essentially, in your backyard and kept absolute silence for four years. Not one of them feeling a bit of remorse, or confessing after too much intimacy with a six-pack."

"Like I said, it's just a theory on my part," said Davis who knew that Fornesby did not get to where he was by being shy when asserting his reservations.

"How was the kid killed?"

"Which one?"

"Either. Both."

"The one four years ago, by a cement block thrown against his head. This new one… I don't know."

"Didn't the family tell you when you met with them?"

"They told me a lot of things, but not that. I'm not sure they were told. The coroner had the remains a long time. I suspect they were fairly decomposed; of course that's why there was suddenly a sinkhole under the pool. Maybe a cause couldn't be determined."

"I sincerely hope that this isn't going to be the table conversation at dinner," said Molly who had picked up on *decomposed* and thought less than *fairly* of it.

"Speaking of football," began Barker in a feigned bragging tone, "I suppose you'd like to swap my Bears for your Browns next fall."

"Never!" replied Davis. "The Browns may be losers, but they're our losers, damn it!"

"Why, Reverend McGowan," chided Beth, "such language!" By now the three couples were gathered into a laughing gaggle. "I think you'll like Marconi's," offered Beth in a decidedly more gracious tone. "It's locally owned and one of our favorites."

Her recommendation proved worthy of the dinner, and the conversation contained nothing grizzly. By the time they had finished, however, the *couples-Fornesby* were heading out of town and back to Cleveland some fifty miles east.

"Davis," Barker gestured him aside as they walked back toward the parking lot. "About our earlier conversation—be careful. Truth isn't always the issue."

Davis understood the reference, and knew this wasn't an introduction to a philosophical debate about ultimate meaning.

"Even if you're right," Fornesby continued, "think about the fact that logic can fall apart when you're talking about local kids from good families whose parents are pillars of the community. Who would you rather send to trial to get a hung jury?"

"A hung jury?"

"Sure. Most people don't need justice as long as they know who they can blame. Put a circumstantial case in front of a jury and hope the defense is not so inept that it can't get it thrown out. The accused gets no jail time, but the community has its answer. They say: *We know who did it, but he got off on a technicality.*"

"I never realized you were so cynical," said Davis knowing full well that every word was potentially real.

"I'm just saying," said Fornesby, "you have a sense of justice that can get you in trouble. Just be careful." He gave a nod toward the four people gathered between two cars. "Molly and I want to hold onto our friends."

Chapter 22

By the Book

It had been a long time since Davis had seen a high school yearbook. His own had been black and white and the yearbook staff's photo-editing capabilities involved scissors to cut around images and contact cement to paste them against white backgrounds.

Computers changed all that. Images were sharp and in color except where artistically faded or swirled or morphed. The seniors' pictures were greatly varied. In his day, the boys, as they were known, wore suits and ties and faced right or left against plain backgrounds. The girls, also in black and white, wore sweaters which were embellished only by a simple charm hanging on a thin chain or a string of pearls. In both cases, only the head and shoulders were visible and uniformity was the rule. The only special effect available was the removal of zits by a steady-handed photo technician with an artist's brush and photographic dyes smeared on a glass plate like a painter's palette.

In Brandon's book, the seniors were set against all sorts of backgrounds and armed with all sorts of props. The net affect was a senior class which consisted of cowboys, mechanics, computer nerds, athletes of every sport and gender, the girl or boy next door, and, from some of the more provocative poses, perhaps future pole dancers for some adult club.

When did I get so old? He mentally tried to calculate the hundreds, maybe thousands, of dollars spent to glamorize a group of ordinary people. The book was also made thicker by a section of ads that could have passed for yellow pages except for a much broader range of color and the fact that business hours and phone numbers played second to slogans like *Keep Rollin' Quarrymen!*

Davis assumed that the sports teams were *The Quarrymen*, and that the name had been used so long that no one heard it as having a gender bias. There was, however, a feeble attempt at political correctness. He noted this when he saw the picture of the women's soccer team under the heading of *The Lady Quarrymen*.

What interested McGowan the most were the comments added in the margins by Brandon's classmates. Several women wrote flirtatiously about wanting to *know the new guy better*, and looking forward to *a great senior year*. These were embellished with smiley faces. One brave soul even dotted her *i's* with hearts. Ashley had written a comment next to a group picture of eighth graders. *You're always #1 with me!* Davis supposed that it was just a nice thing that a sister would write until he went to the varsity football pages. There he found a different interpretation.

The page featured the graduating seniors and cleverly avoided a printed tally of a 3–5 losing season. The scores and schedule were noted, but there were no additional facts. The *Get 'em next year* label, however, visualized the jury's verdict. On the other hand, the slightly smaller individual photos of the stars of the junior class were more positively advertised. The caption beneath Brandon's image read, *Send in the reinforcements!* Someone, however, had written *#2* with a ballpoint pen across his jersey.

McGowan immediately knew the culprit because *#1* was written in the same ink across the chest of Mike Mistrosky. His caption read, *Waiting in the wings!* The only other picture of note showed a line of five thick-necked, serious-expressioned linemen with the caption, *Juniors, all! We'll be back!*

Here was a team with muscle, and with a rivalry that Ashley had described to him earlier. On the page in front of him, it could have been simply the typical male adolescent bravado of two young men vying for first and second string. There were two other things that Davis noted. The first was a hand-printed three-word epithet next to a junior class photo of a young man named Aaron. It read, *Rather be Fishing! (But Fahrenhauser lived in Milan*, thought McGowan. Obviously, he had been in Brandon's school when the Carpenters moved from Tennessee.)

The second item of note was a full page advertisement from The Paradise Pool Company that carried the cryptic message: *Wishing all our teammates the best!* Davis had written checks to that company for years, but now had to admit that he knew precious little about them.

He had borrowed the yearbook to get a picture of the world that the Carpenters lived in. Instead, he felt the animosity of Mike Mistrosky who had been Brandon's obvious rival for the honor of being quarterback in their senior year. Whether by accident or design, no one else from the team had signed the yearbook, but the linemen all had trendy first names coupled with surnames that matched the signs on the county roads. They were Justin, Cramer, Evan, Kyle, and Liam followed by Baumhart, Avery, Huber, Stoutenberg, and Whittlesley. One of the *flip-flops'* last names was *Stoutenberg*, but that may have been a coincidence.

Were the five instructed by the verbal aggression of Mistrosky's pen, or had Brandon closed the book on his teammates? It looked as though it had prompted Ashley's *#1* comment, but it could have been unrelated. *Where were these people now?* Or more importantly: *Where were they the night before the Paradise Pool Company dropped a liner into a hole at the Lexington Glen Condos?*

He studied the sober expressions on the men of the frontline. McGowan could not place any of them on the work crew at the job site. He had been there almost every day and had spoken to all the regulars. On the other hand, Kyle Avery could have been the one who drove a lawnmower-laden pickup truck, but McGowan wasn't sure. His suspicion, however, was confirmed the following day when, after class, Morgan Stoutenberg left the flip-flop middle zone to speak to Davis.

The syllabus indicated that this was to be the term review in preparation for the final exam. The review process always provided confirmation of the early semester hypothesis regarding seat location selection. The front row students might ask for clarification on the difference between Aramaic and Hebrew languages. The students in the middle were more apt to ask if the answers would be all multiple-choice and matching.

"I was wondering if Abby and me could take the final later," began Morgan. Davis gave her the look of one expecting a second round of data.

"I don't know if you are aware of it," she continued, "but the police have discovered the body of a kid that was killed. It's got us really upset. He was on the football team of our high school and my cousin played on the squad with him."

Cynicism is sometimes an emotion that gives too much pleasure, and McGowan avoided slipping into it. In spite of this, the words played through his brain. *Your cousin didn't even sign Brandon's yearbook. The body was Ashley's brother, how do you think she feels? Have you even noticed she's not here?*

"Well," began Davis, "the funeral is tomorrow and the final isn't until next Monday. Will your cousin be there?"

Flip-flop was stunned by her prof's knowing about the service and was unsure of what would be a compelling answer for a question she had not considered.

"I know his dad will be there," she said recovering. "His company put in the pool where they found the body. You can imagine how upset my uncle is."

"Yes," said Davis, "I can imagine. But, I think by Monday we can try to put things back to order, don't you?"

The answer was a blush for a gambit that didn't pay. "I tried," she whispered to Abby who was watching expectantly at the hallway door. Unfortunately, her attempt at whispering was as lame as her con.

"Maybe I'll see you at the funeral," called McGowan after her. This comment registered like a death threat to the pair who now had to consider whether their professor would be taking attendance at an event they had no intention of attending.

Chapter 23

Calling Hours

Davis had *retired* to Huron; he had never actually served a congregation in the area, and so his circle of acquaintances was somewhat limited. Area ministers become well-known to funeral directors who quickly decide whether this new cleric could be a reliable addition to their bullpen and could be called on when an unchurched, grieving family needed someone to conduct a service. At this point in his anonymity, McGowan knew very few morticians and needed Google maps to find the locations of the funeral homes.

The place chosen by the Carpenters was in Monroeville, a city southwest of Norwalk and not within range of his usual east-west driving patterns. The family was scheduled to arrive at 6:30 that evening and calling hours for the public were to run from 7:00 until 9:00. Ashley and her folks thought no one would come, but Davis suspected otherwise. The death of young people always brought out a young crowd riding on the edge of a first awareness of human mortality. He would not have even been surprised if the two *flip-flops* came. Perhaps it would be because of McGowan's closing remark, but it could have been that they did feel some sadness or remorse.

The funeral home itself was located in a very large Victorian house that had been converted to multiple viewing spaces on the first floor and a family apartment above. He parked in the lot behind the green clapboard building. To the south was an open field, a fact that attested that this was, in fact, the very edge of town and on the edge of Ohio's agricultural western frontier.

After seeing that the Carpenters were emotionally settled, Davis added the borrowed yearbook to the display table that the family had assembled showing pictures of the growth of a child to an athletic, happy young man. What was missing were any signs of a casket or a small urn containing the cremains. An explanation came from the funeral director rather than the family.

"It's a very odd situation," said Craig Wheaton who had initially greeted McGowan when he entered the building. "Odd and doubly tragic." Davis wondered what the *doubly* meant but the explanation immediately followed.

"This fellow was one of the quarterbacks that was going to put their high school on the map by taking them to the state finals. Of course he disappeared under strange circumstances and a kid named Mike Mistrosky took over. He was from Winsted, too. He ended up dead in a car accident. *Doubly* tragic."

McGowan recalled the conversation on Kelley's Island following *Golden Willow's* knockdown. "I think I met the people who bought the Mistrosky house," added Davis.

"Losing a kid really messes up a marriage," Wheaton began. This was a small area and people seemed well-versed in everybody else's business.

"What happened that football season?" asked Davis.

"'Bout the same as any other year. They lost about half their games. I guess the Carpenter boy was going to be their secret weapon, but then all that scandal broke out and he was gone."

"You mean about the murder of Aaron Fahrenhauser?"

Wheaton looked up suddenly, apparently taken by surprise at McGowan's knowledge of the players. "Everybody naturally assumed that Carpenter must have been the one."

"The one that did the killing," added Davis.

"Then his body turns up under a swimming pool. Obviously didn't commit suicide, did he?"

"How'd he die?" asked McGowan. With this, Craig fidgeted a bit and looked away.

"The death certificate says *Pending Investigation.*"

"And you have doubts," said Davis trying to draw the man out.

"I've seen the remains," the director continued. "I didn't need any lab tests to know. Obviously, they don't want the information to become public right away."

"They?"

"The police, the people doing the investigation. I'm probably the only one outside a small group who knows what happened."

"And you're not saying," said McGowan.

"I have my own license to protect. When the family asked about it, I just said that the autopsy report would be given later and the cause would be made public."

"Whatever happened to the rest of them?" Davis was changing the subject, and the confusion on Wheaton's face told him that this question had lost his colleague along the way. "The other guys on the football team," he added and Craig's expression lightened. "You know, Kyle Stoutenberg and the others."

"Oddly enough, they're still a team. After high school they went together and started a business. Mistrosky went south to try and play for the OU Bobcats, but they stayed and started a landscape business. Do you know the Stoutenbergs? Everybody thought Kyle would go into his father's pool business, but he stuck with his buddies."

"I don't know Kyle," confessed Davis, "but one of his cousins is one of my students at Firelands."

"Small world, isn't it?" said Wheaton.

Very small, thought Davis who wondered what sort of psychological lock it would take to keep a conspiracy of murder secret for four years in such a tightly knit community. "What's the name of their company?" asked McGowan.

"The Five Linemen! Somehow, it seems appropriate, doesn't it?"

"Sure does," agreed Davis remembering the truth of the caption under their picture in the yearbook, *We'll be back!* They were.

Chapter 24

Free Estimates

It was as Davis suspected. The Carpenters were inundated with people calling at the funeral home and during the service itself. He hoped that most of it was genuine concern from the neighbors that no one really knew rather than the sort of rubbernecking that takes place when people want to see what they were doing with the body. There was, of course, no body at all and the remains of Brandon Carpenter were interred quietly prior to the public event with only the family, Craig Wheaton, and McGowan present. Though he was focused on the service itself, Davis had a sense of a community doing penance for years of assumptions that drained away with the murky water leaking from a swimming pool.

Among the many things that *were* clear in his mind was the suspicion that the details of the murder were known to a group of high school athletes who still referred to themselves as the Five Linemen. His options were not particularly attractive. He could let the whole thing go and stop giving the local police any reason to wonder at his interest in the case. That, however, was not in his nature. Ashley and her family deserved better. Justice deserved truth, but those were his Socratic ideals talking, not common sense.

If he couldn't let it go, he could make a call to Bostwick. Would the cop be moved by a theory of adolescent intrigue and cover-up, or would Davis be accused of trying to shift the lines of suspicion?

A third view seemed, on the surface, the least likely to draw attention from the police or elevate his internal blood pressure. He would call *Five Linemen Lawncare LLC*, and ask for a free estimate. After all, he was retired *and getting up there in years* (at least by the accounts of the very young). The fact was that he did own a lawn, and getting a cost estimate would be counted as normal, rather than extraordinary. He kept the call brief and within the boundaries of the subterfuge.

"Thank you for calling *The Five Linemen*," said a young female voice.

"Is Kyle Stoutenberg there?" said McGowan.

"I'm sorry, Kyle is out on a job; may I help you?" Davis had anticipated the answer, but wanted to interject the name of the person he wanted to see.

"Sure," he said. "My name is Davis McGowan and I live in Huron. I was given Kyle's name and told that he could give me an estimate for a yard work contract. Huron is in your service area, isn't it?"

The conversation was unremarkable in its business details, but exceptional in terms of Davis' real agenda.

"Kyle is working in Berlin Heights this afternoon. He could swing by after that job. Could somebody be at your place at four or four-thirty?"

"That would be perfect," said McGowan who repeated the name and address.

"It might be closer to four-thirty, David."

"That's fine," said Davis not correcting the misunderstood name. There were not a lot of Davises around and it would be better to be written D-A-V-I-D on a memo. Kyle might have read his name in the paper if he had seen the funeral announcement. "I'll just wait if he's a little late, that's fine."

Waiting was never his best game, but it was a part he'd learned to play. It was nearly five when a pickup truck pulled into his drive and a young man with closely cropped blond hair emerged from the cab with a clipboard and a pen. Davis stepped out the door to meet him.

Perhaps it was the memory of mowers in the rear bed that jogged McGowan's memory, but recognition was simultaneous, avoidance, impossible. Had Kyle retreated to the truck, it would only raise questions. The simple thing was to play dumb.

"David McGowan," said Stoutenberg, looking at the clipboard.

"Davis," said McGowan, "the woman who answered the phone must have gotten it wrong–it's a common mistake."

"She said you knew me," he answered hoping that any recognition was one-way.

"Actually, your cousin's in my class at Firelands." (While this was true, it wasn't particularly pertinent.)

"Oh," he said looking around at the yard. "Looks like your lot is sixty-six by one thirty-two." To an outsider it may have sounded like he had an accurate eye for lawn sizes. The truth was that early surveyors in the Northwest Territory were given a thirty-three foot chain as a measuring device. With it, they laid out property lines in rectangles. Here in the old sections of Ohio, the property dimensions were all variables based on the number thirty-three.

"That's right," said Davis. "Do you do snow removal in the winter?" He added this to cut off an easy retreat with words like: *This is too small for us given the travel involved.* It worked to the extent that Kyle walked further up the concrete drive to see if there was a larger paved area behind the house near the garage. He started to take a few notes on the clipboard when McGowan risked the first disclosure.

"You never did send me an estimate when I lived over at Lexington Glen." Stoutenberg froze, and Davis continued. "I met you a few years ago. You acted like you were looking at the landscaping, but I suspect that you were looking at the swimming pool."

"What the fuck!" The explicative told Davis that he had hit a nerve. Confusion or ignorance would have been a better masking response. Swearing meant he was busted.

"Your dad's company installed the liner, the one that covered the body of Brandon Carpenter." The direct approach probably wasn't the brightest, but it was Davis' impulse. He had the man backed into a corner and he would either cower or attack. He studied his victim. He did look like the fellow in the truck at Lexington Glen, but he also could have been in the crowd at calling hours. He would risk pressing the point. "You used the canoe to come up along the ditch from the lake, didn't you?"

"It was an accident," he blurted out, "Mike never meant to shoot him. For God's sake, it was just meant to be a warning shot from a measly .22."

"He was shot?" The revelation took McGowan by surprise, and his response opened a path to escape.

"You're guessing! You don't know a damn thing!" In two-and-a-half heartbeats the pickup was in reverse with Kyle Stoutenberg at the wheel and backing out the drive. McGowan had been guessing. If it really was an accident, he knew nearly nothing. *Why would they go to so much trouble to hide an accident?* On the other hand, he was now past his first guess. He knew something.

Chapter 25

Interest Compounded

Megan Sorento's credentials had made an impression on Sergeant Bostwick, but it was also an unsettling introduction to a cop under pressure to find a reasonable suspect for an old murder. Davis was going to attempt to cash out on an internal bet that the encounter had moved him from a register of possible bad-guys to the good-guy list. Certainly, his conversation with Kyle Stoutenberg had confirmed that the details surrounding the deaths of two high school students four years earlier were known to the founders of Five Linemen Lawncare.

"This is Davis McGowan. Is Sergeant Bostwick there?" The high pitched beep in the earpiece of the phone told him what he had anticipated, that the incoming messages at the Huron Police Department were routinely recorded.

"This is Bostwick, how can I help you?"

"I think you need to talk to the team members that played football with Brandon Carpenter and Mike Mistrosky."

"And why's that?" asked the cop.

"It's a long story, but I thought that I had figured out how the body could have been brought up to the pool."

"You mean, besides the obvious, in the back of a car or truck?"

"You don't understand," began McGowan. "This is a small neighborhood. People almost always look out when a vehicle enters the drive. They would have been seen."

"Would *they*?" asked the cop. "What if the body arrived in a car that they saw all the time? You know—somebody who lived in the development."

This is not the way I wanted this to go, thought McGowan. "Humor me," he said, "I have evidence."

"Okay, convince me."

"Here's what I am thinking: There was an accident out in the spoil area. Instead of calling for help, the guys on the football team pulled together to create a cover-up. They used Aaron Fahrenhauser's canoe to float the body up Washburn Ditch to where the pool was being repaired."

"You think that an *accident* killed those two kids? One by bashing his brains out?"

"I don't know exactly what happened," said Davis who hadn't considered the relationship between the two killings. "I said *accident* because that was the word that Kyle Stoutenberg used when he told me that Brandon was shot with a .22." There was a pause on the city building's side of the connection.

"Look," Bostwick said at last, "we interviewed all the people we thought could have been connected to this. The football team was high on our list, but they were cleared."

"Cleared? How?"

"They *were* all together that night, but south of Norwalk. They were picked up by a deputy from Huron County."

"But they could have gotten there in half an hour," protested Davis.

"You're reaching, McGowan. When the sheriff's department got to them they were pretty much wasted and talking about seeing naked women, not blood. I wouldn't expect you to know this, but there's a gentlemen's club out on Route 250 south of Norwalk. Apparently, a girl that graduated high school a few years ahead of them was dancing there that night, and they wanted to slip into the audience. It was some sort of amateur night, and they told her that they'd cheer from the crowd."

"But they were minors."

"Exactly," said the cop. "They would have just been turned away, but they had already downed a huge dose of beer bravery and were belligerent."

"So the cops were called, how convenient."

Bostwick ignored the attached cynicism and went on. "They would have been turned away even if they hadn't been blotted—half the people in the place knew who they were."

"And they were arrested?"

"No," said Bostwick, "not exactly. Parents were called before anything got out of hand."

"So there were no breathalyzers involved," said Davis.

"None needed. They were all underage and they clearly had been drinking. We didn't need to know their BAC to know that they were violating. None of them was in their cars at the time, so it wasn't a case of DUI."

"So their parents took them home?"

"Look, in that part of the county everybody knows everybody. There'd be a lot of embarrassed families if the thing had gone official. Would have caused a mess of problems for a football coach, too. There was a lot of hype already going on about the next season."

"But, you tell me. Was Brandon shot with a .22?"

"That part, you got right. Did Wheaton tell you?"

"No," said McGowan. "Craig said that *he* could tell the cause from the remains, but that the death certificate said it was still pending. He wasn't allowed to say more than that."

"So, the question for me is how do *you* know that it was a shooting?"

"I told you already," pleaded Davis. "Kyle Stoutenberg said it was an accidental shooting. Mike Mistrosky must have been the one who pulled the trigger."

"Why do you keep saying it was accidental?"

The question stopped Davis. *Accident* was Kyle's word. It was blurted out–so totally unguarded that McGowan had never doubted its truthfulness. It was Bostwick who interrupted his circular thinking.

"A .22 is a dangerous weapon," began the sergeant. "Mostly dangerous because they're treated like toys and given to kids like high-powered bb guns. Sometimes, though, they are the weapon of choice for an assassin. They're small and, as handguns go, pretty quiet when fired. They won't drop an assailant who's headed in your direction, but they'll penetrate the skull when shot point-blank."

"Point-blank?"

"That's how Carpenter was killed–execution style, point-blank to the back of the head. The bullet penetrated but didn't perforate." Bostwick paused to let the words sink in. "You can ask the FBI chick about that, but what it means is that the bullet went in, but didn't come out. It ricocheted through the brain until it finally bounced down into his chest. *Accident* doesn't compute with the forensics."

"I didn't know that," said Davis.

"And, what I don't know is why you said it was a shot from a .22?"

Chapter 26

The Gazebo

McGowan's world was shrinking and it was his own fault. Barker had pegged his shortcomings when he said that Davis was too driven by some idea of justice that wouldn't let this drop. *Truth isn't always the issue*, he had warned.

History was littered with the bodies of those who thought that truth mattered. Socrates had died for it, and Pilate, after playing the politician by asking the crowd who they wanted released, put forward the rhetorical question: *What is truth?* His actions provided the cynical answer that many moderns profess in their creeds: *truth is what people think, or believe, or what they can pass off as reasonable expediency.* None of these fit McGowan. For him, truth meant understanding why a son and brother was dead, even if the facts didn't change anything except moving the name Brandon Carpenter from the list of evil and presumed guilty to the tally of the also dead.

When the phone rang in his living room, his thoughts were still circling inside his head. Nothing in Kyle's blurted confession indicated that the shooting was anything but some sort of accident. Or maybe it was the way he wanted to remember events after four years of playing them out in recall. Bostwick, however, had the actual forensics. The barrel of a small caliber gun had been placed near the back of the head and fired. Assuming it was a handgun, a case might be argued that a group of adolescent boys were playing a game of Russian roulette. That would be odd, stupid, and tragic, but not unheard of, but not to the *back* of the head.

The phone rang for the third time and McGowan emerged from his inner world.

"Hello." An almost imperceptible sigh told him that this was not a computer generated call. "Hello," he said again.

"We have to talk with someone," said a low voice. "The Gazebo at Lakefront—fifteen minutes." The call was over.

McGowan knew what was meant, he just didn't like his options. He could call Darnell or Megan for off-the-record advice, but he already knew what they would say: *Don't go anywhere near the place!* He could bring Bostwick into the encounter, but he might use drawn guns and care more about an arrest than a solution. Who would be arrested, and how would the headline read? *Local citizen arrested in plot to implicate former students!*

Davis had never been known for ranking self-preservation high on his scale of virtues. He had demonstrated this disregard before by giving rides to vagrants, even in the face of admonitions by his colleagues. Still, he was not stupid and needed to think his approach. Literally think his approach.

The Gazebo was in the northeast corner of the park overlooking the small bay and the peninsula which was the spoil area where Aaron Fahrenhauser was found dead. His closest route was to walk north from his house and turn west onto a small road with the overreaching name of Wall Street. That's where they would be watching for him.

Whatever his direction, he would have to walk quite a distance in their plain sight. Still, if he came from the west, it might give him a few steps toward their location before being spotted. Then again, what if they weren't there at all? What if all they wanted was a clear shot of a figure walking across the park with the open skies over the lake as a backdrop? That settled it. He would take a circuitous route by walking west to where South Street curved into a small neighborhood called Sail Away Drive. At one time a place of dilapidated cottage rentals, it was now a picturesque circle of lakefront homes. From there he could swing east and enter the park from behind the shelter of lawn hedges. He would see the gazebo before he had to step into plain view. In any case, fifteen minutes did not allow for any more improvisation, he would be lucky to make the trek around the block as it was. He spoke briefly with Beth, and was out the door.

He wished he'd grabbed a heavier jacket. The sun was the main warmth provider this time of year. The water was cool and the evening chill reminded Davis that the lake was still in suppression mode for higher nighttime temperatures. He wondered if his house was being watched. Kyle knew where he lived, and that suggested going back for a jacket. He found an old one on a hook by the back door and exited to the backyard where he crossed along the abutting property lines, and cut through a neighbor's yard to Center Street. That move would not likely be followed, and he was already a block west of his house and taking an off-street path toward his destination.

The sun had nearly set and the world was dimming fast. He quickened his pace, feeling for the small LED flashlight that he had tucked into his pocket. He needed the last rays of daylight to measure his final approach. He took his position behind an overgrown *Taxus* that sat strategically between the rocky lakeshore and a white house that sat at the road's abrupt and watery end.

He looked across the park toward the rustic square pavilion crowned with a louvered cupola. There were five shapes under its shelter. Two were having an animated discussion with a third. Two others were the watchers. The dimming light might have been playing tricks, but to Davis it looked as if one was facing east down Wall Street, the other south on Center, the most likely paths he would have followed if he had come directly from his home.

A non-descript blue sedan turned their heads as it came down Ohio Street and around the corner of the Episcopal Church. The driver parked slightly at an angle and the headlights momentarily brightened the gazebo. A women enamored with a cell phone conversation got out and immediately turned back toward the church, presumably to the main entrance which faced Ohio Street to the west. It was then that Davis stepped out of the shadows and began to walk across the length of the park. If he had thought about it, he could have calculated the distance in his head. Lakefront Park was a city block wide, two lots deep. In Northwest Territory terms it was eight chain lengths of a survey team, two hundred and sixty-four feet give or take a slight offset and the blacktop of the street in front of him. The distance, however, seemed ten times longer as he stepped out into the lighted street and crossed over to the grassy strand.

To his relief, he was not spotted right away. The five linemen were distracted by the arrival of the car and studied the lone figure until convinced that it was just a parishioner on some volunteer duty. Once satisfied that there was no threat, the two lookouts turned east and south. McGowan was halfway across the span before he heard the hoarse whisper, "There he is."

The five were now at full alert, and Davis tensed. This was his most vulnerable moment. Brandon had been shot execution style with a .22 that would have the report signature of a firecracker or a hard hammer strike on a wooden board. It probably wouldn't alarm the neighbors behind closed doors in a quickly dimming twilight. One of the figures stepped toward him out of the gazebo.

"We thought you might not come," said Kyle.

"I wasn't sure myself," said Davis sounding a cautiousness that may have come too late. Stoutenberg joined the other four by stepping through the opening in the rail that rimmed the shelter. McGowan held back and did not follow the young man into the shadow of the roof. Instead, he kept the square-cut rustic stiles between himself and the five. Even through the camo of the gloom he could make out the features of several faces which had been in the crowd at the funeral home. He already knew their names, but could not attach any to a face besides that of Kyle. The other four were Justin Baumhart, Cramer Avery, Evan Huber, and Liam Whittlesley. Each had at least fifty pounds over McGowan, all of it muscle.

"I assume you want to talk about what happened out there," Davis said nodding to the jutting peninsula, the spoil area that formed the northern perimeter of the bay.

Heads nodded, perhaps with the exception of the one that had been the focus of the animated discussion which he had observed prior to his approach, but only silence followed. They might have been ready to talk, but they had not yet discovered the words.

"You said that it was an accident," said McGowan hoping to engender a response.

"It was," said a new voice followed by a succession of affirmations.

"We were partying on the beach," said the voice that Davis later learned was Cramer Avery's. "Not this one. The one beyond those houses," he added gesturing toward the direction that McGowan had come from.

"West Cove," offered Davis.

"We used to call it Bonfire Bay," said Avery. "We were partying there, nothing too wild. We were celebrating the end of the school and the official beginning of our senior year."

"What changed it? Why did you leave the beach and cross over to the spoil area?"

"We hadn't planned to," said Kyle. "We told Mike to let it go, that it would be Coach's call to make, anyway."

"The coach?" McGowan was not following.

"Liam is better at explaining than I am," confessed Stoutenberg.

"We were all on the football team," said a new voice. It wasn't new information, but Davis nodded as if this level of detail was easier to follow. "Mike, Mike Mistrosky, had been our quarterback since peewee football days, but Brandon moved up here from Tennessee and the adults went bat-shit. *We've finally got a real quarterback*, they said. Made Mike feel like crap. He wasn't bad, but Brandon..."

"Was better." McGowan finished the sentence.

"We told Mike that he might want to try defense," said Justin Baumhart. "He already knew how quarterbacks think; we thought he'd be a great linebacker. He had the speed."

"But how did you end up over there?" asked Davis who was beginning to suspect that the men were walking around the issue rather than moving into an area of painful memory.

"We saw him on his bike," said Liam. "Brandon. He was riding out on the pier. There was no mistaking it. He always rode with a helmet and a backpack. Had orange reflective tape in the shape of a *T*. He was a big Tennessee Volunteer fan. Of course that made everyone mad, too. Around here it's all Ohio State or the MAC Conference. Hey, even if you go to BG or OU, you've still got to be a Buckeye fan."

McGowan nodded.

"Anyway, when he saw Brandon, he said that he wanted to chat with him. Clear the air and all that. He was going to go meet up with him, and did we want to come along."

"Did you go with him?"

"No," said Whittlesley. "If they were going to get into a row, well, we weren't interested in picking sides."

"So you didn't really believe that he was going over to clear the air."

There was a pause for a few moments before Evan Huber entered the conversation. "It wasn't that we didn't believe him, at least not me. Mike was… well, hotheaded. He might have wanted to bury the hatchet, but we also knew that he could lose it in a minute."

"So why didn't you go with him?" Davis repeated.

"He'd have expected us to side with him," said Stoutenberg. "For him everything was about loyalty. You were on his side or you were on the other guy's side."

"And you weren't taking sides."

"Exactly. It was between the two of them. It was really stupid. Coach would decide who was going to be in the huddle."

"Did you know he had a gun?"

"We should have," said Baumhart. "He always carried his little pea shooter, as he called it, at least when we came anywhere near the lake."

"Why's that?"

"Snakes," offered Liam. "He was petrified of snakes. They're really bad in early spring."

McGowan nodded. He had often seen tangles of them caught up in the frenzy of the mating season. The mating balls were alarming to see, but harmless to all except perhaps the poor female whose pheromones had baited a couple dozen male suitors.

"They're mostly not poisonous," he offered.

"Didn't matter. They really creeped him out. We should have known he had the gun, but we didn't think about it."

"So he went over by himself. What happened after that?"

"We're just here by ourselves, keeping pretty quiet so that the neighbors wouldn't call the cops."

"In other words, you were drinking," said Davis.

"We had two six-packs between us; that's all. We weren't going to get busted for drinking. Coach would have killed us."

"But you did get busted for drinking later that night," said McGowan. The five looked at each other wondering how much else this stranger knew. Kyle had told them of the slip about an accidental shooting, but this outsider had information about other events of the evening. Still, they had seen this man standing with the Carpenters at the casket, and felt he might help them heal from a wound on the verge of becoming gangrenous. Brandon's body had been discovered and the shared secret was now public. The runaway teen quarterback had not run at all.

"One beer," said Justin. "We each had one beer before Mike left. We said we'd hold off on our second until he came back. There were six of us and we had them all counted out. We ditched the cans in the high grass in case the cops came by and told him that he had half an hour, or we'd drink his, too."

"So you gave him an incentive to return."

"We were having a little team night out, not a fight."

"What changed that?"

"We knew that we hadn't given him much time. By the time he hoofed it around the shore to where Brandon had dragged his bike into the grass, he'd almost have to turn around to make it back. But he came back in a canoe. He said that he had seen something terrible, and he didn't know what to do."

"What did he see?"

"He said he came up through the brush and heard Aaron and Brandon arguing. He came up on them quietly because he didn't know what was going on. Anyway, he said he saw Brandon haul off and hit Farhrenhausen across the skull with a cement block. We said that we should go to the police, but he said it was worse than that.

"He had his peashooter, so he pulled it out and called to Carpenter to stand still. He said that Brandon was still really raging and started for him. He tried to fire a warning shot, but the guy dove right into the line of fire. Bullet hit him in the head. He was dead."

"We still said we should call the police," offered Kyle. "But Mike said that he would be the one who looked guilty. After all, he was the one with the gun. It was a frickin' little .22 and shouldn't have that much power."

Depends on proximity to the barrel, thought Davis remembering Bostwick's description of the forensics. *Execution style* had been his exact words. *Did these five know or guess that Mistrosky was lying?* "What did you do, then?" he asked.

"Cramer and I got into the canoe with him and rowed back," said Liam. "The others ran the long way around. When we got there it was a mess—a lot of blood, mostly Airhead's."

"Airhead?"

"Sorry," said Liam, "it's the nickname we used with Aaron. He was one of those brainiacs who was good at a lot of things, but never quite got the social scene.

"Mike was right. The place was such a mess that no one would ever have been able to figure out what had happened. He would have been blamed. It was his gun that killed Brandon; who was to say that he wasn't the one who hit Aaron with the damned brick."

That's what I might think, thought Davis. "What happened to the gun?"

"We told him to ditch it. He threw it off the pier into the river. It's deep there."

They keep it deep, thought McGowan. *Every few years they dredge the channel for the ore boats. If it was thrown there four years ago, it's probably long gone. Been scooped into a barge with the farmland silt and dumped far offshore.*

"Why did you say that it was mostly Aaron's blood?"

Davis became aware of the wave movement on the nearby water. The lake was quiet and relegated to a rhythmic *tissh-tissh*, but that soft sound seemed amplified by the long silence under the small pavilion.

"The bullet went into his head, but it didn't come out."

Again, the wavelets punctuated the moment.

"How did you know that he was dead?" Davis broke in on the stillness.

"No heartbeat, no breathing, no nothing. The bullet must have hit him just right, or just wrong. It was an accident. But after what he'd done to Air… Aaron, it seemed like he got what he deserved."

"So you helped get rid of the body."

"None of us even wanted to look at it, but we loaded it into Aaron's canoe and moved it back over to where we had been partying. No one was there, and we thought we'd take it up that little stream and dump it where no one would find it."

Liam's words confirmed McGowan's suspicions. "But they would have found it eventually," he said.

"Kyle went across with Mike in the canoe," continued Whittlesley. "The rest of us went around the long way, and we collected Brandon's bike. We had the idea that if Carpenter had run away, he'd use the bike for speed."

"Who decided to bury him under the pool?"

"I realized where we were," said Kyle softly. "My dad's company was scheduled to put in a liner at those condos. We started up the creek and pretty soon we were in an open space beyond Cleveland Road. Well, it hit me that I knew exactly where we were and that it wasn't all that far to the worksite."

"But you weren't part of the work crew that summer?" said Davis.

"No, I wasn't," said Kyle. "I worked all that summer out of Mansfield. I only knew about this job because I got back to Norwalk early the day before and my father sent me in a van to deliver the liner. When I got there, I saw the setup. Hell, I knew the whole drill. They'd drop the liner in the morning because it would take a full day to get enough water to make sure it was set properly.

"I went on ahead of the boat crew to make sure the way was clear. There were some security lights, but I saw how we could stay clear of any direct light. I had a hole excavated before they got the canoe up from the creek."

"That was the hardest thing I'd ever done," said Cramer Avery. "In the end we just portaged, the water was deep enough, but it was running too fast."

An African would find a way, thought Davis whose mind suddenly ran to the personal resilience that he saw in the people of Kenya. "So you used the canoe to carry the body?"

"We all helped," continued Cramer. "I think we were running on anger for what he had done to Fahrenhauser, and afraid of what might happen to Mike if he was arrested."

"So Kyle covered the body and fixed all the scars on the surface so that the workers wouldn't suspect anything the next day," said McGowan.

"We had to keep quiet," said Stoutenberg, "so I sent them back with the canoe, finished my work, and walked out to the street. It must not have taken long to ride the canoe downstream because they were back soon. They had the bike in the trunk and Mike said that he thought we should go somewhere and make a scene—somewhere far from the lake, that way people would remember seeing us. We took the beer so that we could chug it later and smell like we'd been drinking."

"So you went to see a girl you knew at a strip club," said Davis. The five didn't know how to react to the sudden revelation that McGowan knew more than he was saying. "And, you dumped the bike near an exit ramp onto 250 south of Norwalk, a place where Carpenter might have hitched a ride out of the area."

The group's reaction made Davis hesitate. *Would they think he had been baiting them?* If they did, they did not get any time to react. A patrol car pulled up next to the sedan that had been parked under the streetlight. The policeman got out and shined a flashlight into the car's interior. Seeing nothing, he turned toward the lake scanning for figures faintly lit by the amber glow of the cityscape.

"McGowan?" It was Sergeant Bostwick and a bright beam crossed over Davis' face causing him to quickly look away.

"You ratted us," said one of the five.

"No, I didn't," whispered Davis. "This guy has been on my case. He's after me, not you."

"The park is supposed to be cleared at sundown," said the cop.

"Sorry," said McGowan. "When we started chatting it was still light. Guess we just got carried up in the discussion. We'll leave now."

"Who's with you?"

"Just a couple of guys from my class over at Firelands. I bumped into them and we just got talking."

"Well, clear out. You don't want to be arrested for something as dumb as loitering, not with your history." Bostwick turned back to the patrol car.

The five were equally quick to scatter toward wherever they had left their vehicles. Davis presumed that they were parked nearby, but out of sight.

"Kyle," he called. The young man turned toward him. "What are you going to do?"

"Besides not sleep?" he answered. "I don't know. None of us can live like this. Mike is dead, you know. He was doing weird things before his accident. He sent a postcard to Ashley when he was down visiting campus at OU. We asked him why he was messing around with something that was an accident."

"And it made you think." McGowan realized that he had never looked at a map to see that Lake Hope State Park was near to Athens and Ohio University where Mistrosky wanted to play ball. The postcard had come from there.

"It made all of us wonder why would he risk getting caught trying to frame a guy who he knew was guilty and dead, besides?"

"Unless Brandon wasn't guilty... is that what you thought?"

"What would you do, Dr. McGowan?"

"I'm not the one in this situation," said Davis, "but if the police suspect what you are now guessing, then this isn't a bunch of guys covering for a friend, and the longer you wait, the worse it'll get. I think you need a lawyer. Tell your story and let your counsel go with you to the police. It won't be easy."

"It hasn't been already," said Kyle who turned and ran into the darkness.

McGowan's next awareness was the chill in the air as he turned and walked toward the lonely blue car. He pulled his LED flashlight from his pocket and clicked it quickly on and off. The headlamps of the sedan answered back as Beth stepped out of the shrubbery near the corner of the brick church building.

"This is the worst thing you ever had me do," she said. "I about died when the cop started to look at our car. Why would he do that? It wasn't illegally parked."

"That was Sergeant Bostwick," replied Davis, "and I now suspect that he's put some sort of GPS tracking device on my car. He doesn't know, but he became my backup."

"I thought that's what I was doing," said Beth. She held a cell phone in one hand and the remote control key ring for Davis' car in the other.

"Well, he upstaged you tonight. I'm glad you were here, though. If they had turned on me, one flash of light would have made them think they were being monitored. It turned out that I'm the one being watched."

"What did they say?"

"They were there, but I think they really believed that Brandon was shot by accident. They were just helping a friend."

"Will the authorities believe that?"

McGowan paused. "I don't know. I didn't tell them anything about the gun being fired point-blank. If they tell everything they know, their interrogators will know that they really don't know everything. They weren't there when it happened. I told them to get an attorney."

"Somebody smart, I hope," she said.

"I think I'll call Darnell and Megan. Bet they'll know who would be able to talk to them and protect them."

"I think you're right. What do we need to do now?"

"Well, if Bostwick is to be believed, I'd better get home before I'm arrested for violating my curfew. How about a steaming hot cup of tea?"

"And a hot bath!"

Chapter 27

On Patrol

There are many heralds of early spring, but the absolute confirmation takes place when weekly lawn mowing goes into full force by the end of March. The red gas can in McGowan's garage was nearly emptied by late May and, as he raked the clippings, he wondered again why he thought fertilizing was a good idea.

As a promise to Beth, he had sworn off any more interference with a police investigation. This was, however, only after Megan Sorento had given him a name of someone who could represent a confused group of young men who were being twisted by memories of events that they did not yet understand. Both Megan and Darnell were truth seekers, but they also understood how circumstances sometimes bent time and space. "From everything they said," Davis confided, "they were accessories after the fact, probably duped by friendship and adolescent loyalty." That continued to be his assessment, even now that he was off the case by direct order of a wife who sat in the bushes and hoped that flashing car lights might make potential ruffians think again about making her a widow.

In all fairness, McGowan had every intention of keeping his word as he lifted a damp green pile of fresh mowings into a brown paper refuse bag. His failure began when, out of the corner of his eye, he saw a black and gray car coming down the street. In the old days, his habit was to look up and wave at one of Huron's finest. Now, he didn't know what to do. Looking busy and overworked seemed the safest option. When the car slowed and turned into his driveway, he had to look, but he already knew that it would be Bostwick.

"Can we talk?" said the sergeant through his rolled down window.

For Davis, it was a bad opening line because it played into one of those husband-and-wife games that came of being old enough to remember good grammar. Of course the correct answer to *Can we talk?* is *I don't know, are you able?* but the punch line would be lost to most people under fifty, maybe fifty-five. Instead, he held his normal response, set aside the rake and said, "Sure."

The car door opened and the tall man uncoiled himself to stand alongside Davis who suddenly felt like he had swallowed some shrinking potion. "Do you want to come inside?" asked Davis.

"No," said the cop. "This won't be long and it's off the record. Let's just get a little away from the street, if that's okay." Bostwick's tone seemed remarkably conciliatory considering their last encounter. "You know," he said, "we cracked the case."

"Which case was that?" said an intentionally dense McGowan preferring this rendition of the cop. They both laughed.

"For what it's worth," said Bostwick, "no one in the department ever thought that you were in on anything. What we did know is that you were onto something and were getting information in places where we were getting blank stares."

"So is that why you were keeping tabs on my car? I mean, you drove straight up to it a few nights ago."

Bostwick smiled. "Thanks for reminding me. Can I get back the department's tracking unit that's been hitchhiking with you for the last couple of weeks?"

I don't know, are you able went the brain tape, but the mouth said, "I suspected something like that."

"We wanted to know who was talking to you, and, I'll add, you were doing dangerous stuff. This was clearly a double murder."

"I'm not sure the five linemen knew that part of the story."

"That's what I have to ask you about. Those five are tight. They played football together. They started a company together. They hauled a dead body half a mile upstream and buried it in your backyard."

"And I think it's become more of a guilt burden than a bunch of seventeen-year-olds might have guessed when they went to help their friend," added Davis.

"That's what I have to ask you about. I know that you were talking to them in the park the other night. What did they say? What did you say? They've had a lot of time to get a story together."

McGowan considered the questions before answering. "I don't think this has been something that they've talked about a lot. The other night, it was like they were reliving it for the first time in a long time. I told them nothing about what I learned from you. They were insistent that the shooting was entirely an accident. They believed, at the time, that their friend, Mike, had seen a horrendous murder. He had shot in self-defense, and he would look guilty because it was his gun. They acted like a team, and defended their quarterback."

"Why do you say, *at the time*? Is it different now?"

"Some are thinking that way. They knew that Brandon and Aaron were friends, and they had met to spend an evening fishing. Their buddy Mike seemed to disintegrate after it all happened. Didn't make it in college, sent a bogus postcard, drank until high speed and a bend in the road put him out of his misery. Meanwhile, at least, Kyle used to come back to look at the swimming pool. I think they were afraid that they might have gotten it wrong, but there was no way to fix it. I don't think they were bad kids. Not really."

"So you're wondering what will happen when the autopsy is made public and it says that the barrel of the gun was pressed against the skull," said Bostwick.

"It was? You mean, actually in contact with his head?" asked Davis.

"Hard to use the accident excuse, isn't it?"

"Maybe Mistrosky crept up to him and stuck it to the back of his head as a joke, but it went off by mistake," suggested McGowan.

"Those little .22 caliber pistols are notoriously hard to pull, unless the hammer is cocked. Of course, we don't have the gun."

"And won't," said Davis. "What'll happen to them?"

"I think a deal is in the works. It'll test their grit, though. They'll plead guilty to accessory after the fact, and have to face the Carpenters. They were all minors at the time, but probably would have been tried as adults. I suspect that, under the circumstances, they'll get suspended sentences with probation and community service. I can handle that as long as I know that they're not just playing out a story."

"I don't think they are," said Davis. "It's going to test a whole lot of things, their friendship, their business, their families…"

"I got to give them credit," said the cop, "they covered their bases pretty well, had their parents baffled with underage drinking, and trying to get into a strip club."

"Two beers," said McGowan, "they had two beers each. They didn't want to get busted and make the coach angry."

"We respond to family disputes all the time where some abusive person blames the beer for his wife's fat lip. *The beer defense* we call it. Here, they actually pulled it off. What are the two things that people would automatically assume is true about what happens when a handful of juvenile macho guys get together? They drink beer and try to see girls naked!"

"Exactly," said Davis. "And I wish it was true on that night."

"Well, evidently the mayor's thinking about giving a commendation to the department for solving the case."

"Well, that's good news," said McGowan. "Congratulations!"

"We both know it's pure bullshit," said Bostwick. "Thanks."

"I'm just glad not to get that loitering ticket."

"A couple of other things," began the sergeant. "*Can I call on you again?* You know, if I get stumped about something–off the record, of course?"

Good thing I'm not in the grammar squad. "Sure, always glad to help. You said a couple of things. What else?"

"It's your wife," said the cop. "Try to keep her from hiding in the bushes. It's a little creepy." They both laughed.

"Actually," said Davis, "she was supposed to be my back-up. Then you arrived."

"That reminds me, I need to get that tracking unit."

Chapter 28

One Nervous Cop

Outdoor weddings present strategic challenges for brides and grooms intent on maintaining traditions like not seeing the bride until she walks down the aisle. For one thing there is no real aisle other than the one defined by white folding chairs from the florist. There are no curtains or doors or any other convenient architectural structures from which the groomsmen appear. The lakefront at Sawmill Creek is a grassy lawn which ends in a bank of riprap that breaks the oncoming surf.

Darnell was a basket case and his best man, a retired cop named Jake Sobieski, was earning his pension by keeping the groom calm. Though they kept the *can't see the bride* tradition intact, other customs had come crashing down. One of the grooms*men* was introduced to Davis as Ronnie Matheny, but her real name was probably Veronica. As a counterpoint perhaps, one of Megan's attendants was Bruce McClelland. Megan's parents were on the bride's side, but Wilson had a Ms. Brown as his honorary mother.

Sorento was nowhere to be seen. Actually, the women were to be delivered to the service in two limousines, the first with the attendants, the second with the bride and her father. The fantasy that this was meant to capture meant that McGowan would have to hoof it quickly between the nervous groom and the women who were behind a line of pine trees a hundred yards away. It was his old routine which was now complicated by geography. He always made a final round with the man and woman in order to go over the vows and confirm all the little niceties from the rehearsal that might have fallen from the frontal cortexes.

"Darnell, relax," said Jake as McGowan approached. "You're marrying Megan, for God's sake! What's to be nervous about?"

"Them," he said pointing to the growing crowd.

"Just forget about them," offered Davis. Just then there was an audible hush from the throng and the sounds of the string quartet finally made it back to where the groom and his friends now huddled. They looked to see the reason for the sudden quiet when an unidentified voice announced it.

"It's a bald eagle." It was flying just offshore along the waterline in the same flight path that they had seen from *Golden Willow* on the Sunday when the McGowans took the couple sailing.

"There," said Jake, "what could be a better sign than that for you two?" Whether or not that was the reason, Darnell ceased his fidgeting, and Davis felt okay about leaving him in order to find the sequestered bride's team.

He passed behind the congregation which was now settling into their seats. It's always a precarious moment outdoors when people take to the wooden seating. If the ground is too saturated from recent rain, the front staves of the chair legs dig into the soggy turf creating uneasiness for those fearing that movement of any sort would send them deeper and deeper into the turf. But the ground was solid and there were no suddenly surprised looks from people taking their seats. In his rush, he noticed a young woman in a silver metallic dress handing out bulletins. He probably would not have paid any attention at all were it not for the fact that she also sported a tinseled fascinator that was woven into her dark hair.

Fascinators were not new to McGowan. They were often worn by women in the U.K. He usually saw them, however, in services where the male guests wore kilts, the official tuxedo of Scotland. Still, Will and Kate's wedding had brought the awareness to the colonies, and he suspected it would soon be trendy in the U.S.

The bride was in better condition than the groom, and her support group was chatting easily. They, too, had seen the eagle's flight, but Sorento greeted Davis with quite a different topic.

"Did you see Ashley Carpenter?" she asked.

"No," said McGowan, "did you invite her to the wedding?"

"Better than that, I asked her to hand out bulletins. She said she would surprise me, and she did. I think your lady in black has a little life in her."

Davis stepped out of the shadow of the trees and looked back toward the gathered guests. The early evening sun sparkled on the water and on the silver plumes of a once Goth-girl's headdress. "Thank you," he said to Megan.

Washburn Ditch

There's a place where the ditch
cuts under the highway
and great pipes carry the flow,
channeling the flood until
it bursts free meandering
to reclaim its older path.

From there, earth is cut away
by water snaking around
dipping under fallen trunks
sidling past the heaps of brush
that washed down from neighborhoods
on the other side of town.

Floating toys will take the ride
before fast grip can gather,
escaping backyards during
the sudden-rising storm surge.

Here in the wooded silence,
beyond the noisy traffic,
they pile up in the tangles
waiting rescue that won't come.
The squirrels take no notice,
and muskrat finds no delight.

In the purgatory
of lost objects they pass time
until other hands find them,
or greater floods send them on.

from *The Immigrant's House* by Rob Smith

Rob Smith currently lives and writes on Ohio's north coast. He enjoys sailing, and when not working on his novels, he is refurbishing an 1850's house which was built by a ship's carpenter turned lighthouse keeper. In addition to his prose, he is also known for his poetry. In 2006 he won the Robert Frost Poetry Award from the Frost Foundation in Lawrence, MA. He holds his undergraduate degree from Westminster College in Pennsylvania and master and doctoral degrees from Princeton Theological Seminary.

Davis McGowan made his first appearance in *McGowan's Call* which was published in 2007.

To learn more about the author, visit his website at: SmithWrite.net

PHOTO CREDIT:
NANCY SMITH

CPSIA information can be obtained
at www.ICGtesting.com
Printed in the USA
FFOW02n1828160415
12697FF